GENTLE HAND

PERFECT HANDS SERIES BOOK TWO

NORA PHOENIX

Gentle Hand (Perfect Hands series book two) by Nora Phoenix. Copyright ©2019 Nora Phoenix

Cover design: Vicki Brostenianc www.vickibrostenianc.com

Editing: M.A. Hinkle

Proofreading: Tanja Ongkiehong

All rights reserved. No part of this story may be used, reproduced, or transmitted in any form by any means without the written permission of the copyright holder, except in case of brief quotations and embodied within critical reviews and articles.

This is a work of fiction. Names, characters, places, and incidents either are the products of the author's imagination or are used fictitiously. Any resemblance to actual persons, living or dead, businesses, companies, events, or locales is entirely coincidental. The use of any real company and/or product names is for literary effect only. All other trademarks and copyrights are the property of their respective owners.

This book contains sexually explicit material which is suitable only for mature readers.

www.noraphoenix.com

PROLOGUE

Five Years Earlier

"What's wrong, Raf?"

He was a total wuss, of course, for tearing up all over again at that simple question. It was just that Rhys's voice was so warm and understanding, like it always was. The guy had the patience of a saint to put up with him. Fuck knew he was one of the few people who did.

"Raf?" Rhys said, putting a hand on his shoulder.

Raf leaned into his touch, as he so often did. It helped Raf focus, that simple hand on his shoulder. Rhys was good with the touching thing, not caring if others thought it was weird or gay. He was out and proud, though not loud, as he always told Raf. To Rhys, being gay was who he was, and he saw no need to shout it from the rooftops. Rhys went about his life and ignored the occasional homophobic remark slung his way, something Raf desperately wanted to learn from him.

Not that he was out. God, no. He wanted to be, if only because pretending was so damn exhausting, but he couldn't. He had to graduate first and be off to college, away from his father. There was no telling how the man would react to Raf coming out, though his guess was the meltdown would be of catastrophic proportions.

But he was getting distracted again instead of telling Rhys what was going on. Right. *Focus, Raf.*

"I got the diagnosis," he said, raising his eyes and meeting those of his best friend, Rhys. Hell, his *only* friend. Many people liked him at first sight, but it never seemed to last. Rhys was the only one who'd stuck with him, and he didn't even make it feel like it was a sacrifice. Raf felt that Rhys genuinely liked him, which was amazing and baffling at the same time.

Rhys lowered himself onto the bleachers next to him, where Raf had found a spot, pretending to be watching the cheerleaders practice. Their slim bodies twisted and turned, their faces always smiling as they practiced their tumbling and complicated routines. He'd watched them for a long time, his mind going to a hundred different places.

He sat here often, their practices somehow a comforting routine for him that beat the hell out of going home. No one looked at him twice on those bleachers. The cheerleaders barely noticed him anymore by now. Not that anyone believed him to be interested in girls in the first place. Still, it was all part of the pretense he had to keep up, at least until he graduated. If he even stood a chance at graduating after this. God, high school sucked.

Rhys's hand found his and gently squeezed it. *Right. Focus.* Raf had to explain. "ADHD. That's what I have.

ADHD. They can give me pills or something, which can help, but that's it."

"It's not the end of the world. Those meds can be very effective, so they may help you function much better than you do now. Get more sleep, maybe, be able to focus better."

Raf looked sideways at Rhys, who studied him with kind eyes. "You don't sound surprised."

"I'm not. It's not uncommon, you know, and I've had a suspicion for a while now."

Raf slowly shook his head. "You never said anything."

"No, because we both know that would've not gone over well. I'm your friend, not your fucking counselor or doctor, and I'd like to keep it that way."

As much as Raf hated to admit it, Rhys had a point there. "Sorry," he mumbled, a little embarrassed. It wasn't the first time he wished he was more like his best friend, and it wouldn't be the last time either.

"What did your parents say?"

Boy, *there* was a loaded question. Raf cringed as he remembered his father's reaction. He'd always been of the yelling variety, but that outburst had taken it to a whole new level. "My mom was very sweet and understanding," he offered, but of course, Rhys could read between the lines. He always did.

Rhys's eyes softened as he put a hand on Raf's thigh. "Wanna come hang out at my place for the weekend? My mom is away with some friends on a wine-tasting weekend or some shit, so it's just me and my dad."

Raf nodded instantly, gratitude flooding him.

"Awesome. Let's leave your car here, and I'll drop you off Monday morning."

Raf let out a sigh. It was so much better when someone else made those practical decisions for him.

"You know what's so frustrating?" he asked a few minutes later when they were driving to Rhys's house. "When my dad gets so angry with me, it only makes things worse. Thinking is hard enough for me as it is, but when he starts yelling, it's like my brain shuts down. I become this stuttering, fumbling idiot who can't string two coherent sentences together and who drops everything he touches."

Rhys's right hand left the steering wheel for a second and squeezed his thigh again. "I know. Just a few more months, Raf, and then you're off to college."

Raf bit his lip. "What if my grades aren't good enough? What if I don't get accepted because of this?"

Rhys shot him a quick look sideways. "There are many guys like you who get into college. If they'd reject everyone with ADHD, they'd have barely anyone left."

A smile broke through on Raf's face. "That's BS, but I appreciate the sentiment."

"You'll get into college, I promise," Rhys said.

Raf sighed. "You always have more faith in me than I have in myself. God, sometimes I wish I could love you, you know?"

Rhys brought a hand to his heart and faked being shot. "Are you saying my undying love is unrequited? You've mortally wounded me!"

Raf grinned. Rhys was so funny and sweet at the same time. "You know what I mean."

"Yeah, you're saying that if I were twenty years older, you'd totally do me."

"Dude, if I were twenty years older, you'd be all over me," Raf fired back.

They grinned at each other, both comfortable knowing what they liked. Oh, they'd kissed once, back when their friendship was new and they discovered they were both gay, but they'd agreed that had been an experiment they would never, ever repeat. Nope, they shared an affinity for older men and were unashamed about it—at least to each other.

"Oh, Cornell is here." Rhys pointed at the car that belonged to Cornell Freeman, his father's best friend. Raf, who wasn't the most perceptive, noticed an edge to his voice. Usually, he would've blurted something out about Rhys *liking* him, but because Rhys had been amazing enough to offer him a safe haven for the weekend, he held back. With effort, because holy crap, Rhys liking his dad's best friend was *interesting*.

"Nice," he said because he had to say something, and dammit, Cornell *was* nice.

Rhys's father—Jonas—and Cornell were hanging out on the deck with a couple of cold beers, the barbecue already fired up. Their conversation stopped abruptly when Rhys and Raf walked in. What had they been talking about?

"Hey, Dad," Rhys said. "Is it okay if Raf stays with us for the weekend?"

Jonas's eyes were kind as he sent Raf an encouraging smile. "Sure. It's always a pleasure to have you around, Raf."

Now, why the fuck couldn't he have a dad like that?

"Thank you." It was the polite thing to say, even if he knew it wasn't needed here. They wouldn't ream him out here if he forgot to say thank you, or forgot to turn the lights off, or forgot to close the garage door, or forgot any of the hundred things he was supposed to remember, but his brain refused to.

"Hey, Cornell." There was that edge again in Rhys's voice. Raf bit his lip from saying anything. because that would be unforgivable.

"Hey, kiddo," Cornell said, shooting both of them a lazy smile. Gah, he was hot with his lean body, those gray hairs that peppered his dark hair, and a pair of blue eyes that were always kind. Then again, Jonas wasn't bad looking either, though Raf would never admit that to Rhys. There were things you shouldn't say about someone's dad, that much even he knew.

"We'll be in my room, Dad," Rhys announced.

"I'm making ribs, so come down in an hour or so 'cause they'll be ready," Jonas said.

"Cornell is hot," Raf said as soon as they were in Rhys's room, his attempt at being poking him a little to see what he could stir up. Rhys, of course, saw straight through him.

"You picked up on that?" he said with a hint of panic. "Oh god, I hope he didn't notice. If you saw, that means I wasn't being very subtle about it. Crap."

Raf's face broke open in a wide smile. "You *really* like him." He kept his voice low.

Rhys rolled his eyes at him but then settled himself on his bed, with Raf finding a spot to lounge on the floor like he usually did. He could never sit long anyway, and the floor offered more room to move.

"I do." Raf felt a flash of triumph that he'd called it. "But please, promise me you won't say anything to anyone. It's crazy. He's my dad's best friend, and he's way too old for me. It's just a crush."

Raf held up both hands with his index and middle finger crossed. "I swear. I know my filter malfunctions often, but I'd never embarrass you like that. But why would he be too old? I thought you liked older guys?"

Rhys let out a groan. "Yeah, I know. It's just... I *really* like him, and it's annoying because he'll never see me as more than his best friend's kid, you know? He's known me since I was a baby."

"He's single, though, right? And gay?" Raf was proud he

could remember Rhys had told him as much, even if the exact details were lost on him.

Rhys nodded. "His boyfriend dumped him after cheating on him. I heard my mom and dad talk about it."

"Poor guy." Raf spared a short thought for his father, who he'd seen banging their neighbor, the one with the fake tits that didn't even bounce when she played tennis. She was nice enough, though a little too perky and happy for his taste, and she baked the best chocolate chip cookies in the world, but he didn't get what his dad saw in her or why he had to cheat on his mom like that. Then he shrugged. Not his problem, and he wasn't stepping into that mess, if only out of sheer survival instinct.

"You never know what could happen," Raf said. "Things can change."

As cliché as it was, it did seem to cheer Rhys up a bit. "You're right. I shouldn't give up."

That made Raf sad, for some reason. Maybe it was because he knew that even if Rhys didn't end up with Cornell—and he had to admit the chances were slim—he'd find someone else who was great and perfect for him. There was no way a guy like him would stay single.

"Who would ever want me?" he said, the sadness flooding him now. "I'm such a hot mess."

Rhys lifted a single eyebrow. "Yeah, with the emphasis on *hot*. Have you seen your ass lately? Dude, give it time. You'll find your way through this diagnosis, through life. You just have to find how and where you fit in."

"What if I don't fit anywhere?" Raf asked, his voice trembling a little. "The only person I've ever felt at home with is you. What if I'll never find that with anyone else?"

Rhys lowered himself onto the floor on his belly as well,

their faces close. "If I tell you a secret, can you promise me to never, ever tell anyone?"

Raf nodded instantly, but Rhys put his hand on Raf's. "I'm serious. This is not something you can blurt out at any given time, okay?"

Raf hesitated at Rhys's serious tone, then nodded again, but much more slowly. "I promise."

"I think my parents are getting a divorce."

Raf's eyes widened. "Oh no!" he whispered.

"But that's not even the secret. I've found out that they're in an unusual relationship. They're Domme and submissive."

This time, Raf's mouth dropped open, and he didn't close it until drool pooled in his mouth. "They're *what*?"

"My mom is a Domme, and my dad is her submissive. And Cornell is a submissive as well."

Talk about a bombshell. Raf shook his head, something he often did to force himself to follow one line of thought and not let the chaos in his head overwhelm him.

"So your mom, like, whips your dad and stuff?" he asked, his voice filled with awe.

"I don't know what they do exactly, but maybe? Not sure I want to know. But I overheard them talking about it when they didn't know I was home."

Yeah, Raf wasn't sure he wanted more details either. Sex was weird enough to think about, let alone sex like that. And yet, at the same time, the idea tickled him. "How do you know they're getting a divorce?"

Rhys's face grew tight. "They're always fighting lately," he said softly. "It's not much fun to be around them. They pretend everything is fine, but it's not. I think they're waiting for me to graduate and leave for college."

Raf leaned in and rubbed Rhys's hand against his cheek. "I'm sorry. That must make you sad."

"It does, but this fighting drives me crazy as well, so by now, I'm over it."

"But why did you tell me this? Not the divorce thing, but the whole Domme/sub thing."

"Because I thought you'd find comfort in knowing that even if it turns out you don't fit in with the vanilla folks, there's a whole world for you to explore."

1

He was getting too old for this. Brendan sighed as he found a quiet spot in one of the club's booths where he could sip his Coke and contemplate his social life. Or lack thereof, as fate would have it. The club was busy enough for a Saturday evening, and he'd spotted a number of boys he'd played with before as well as some cute-looking newbies, but he wasn't feeling it.

He'd known it for a while, but tonight had made it clear. At forty-three, he was done playing. Weekends in the club, the occasional boy who wanted something more for a few weeks or a few months, it no longer appealed to him. He wanted a boy to call his own, someone to wake up with and tuck into bed every night. His house was ready for it, a gorgeous room awaiting the perfect boy...but Brendan was losing hope he'd ever find him.

Oh, he'd thought he had when he'd met Henry, but that had turned out to be nothing but heartbreak. It had made him gun-shy to even try again, and for a while he'd stuck to quick encounters in the club. But that wasn't him, and it wasn't what he wanted. The question was: would he find what he was looking for in the club? It seemed doubtful, but where else could he meet someone who was into the same things as him?

He took another sip of his Coke, then sank lower in the booth and closed his eyes for a second. These booths were perfect if you wanted a little privacy, whether for yourself or because you wanted to engage in some *activities* without everyone watching. Though in this club, someone was always watching. That was kind of the point. If you didn't want that, there were private rooms available.

"I'm sorry, Rhys." A crystal-clear, young voice carried over from the booth next to him. "I tried, I swear. I really tried."

"I know. Don't worry about it," someone else said, his voice a bit more hushed. Rhys, Brendan assumed, since that's what the other voice had called him. The name sounded familiar, but he couldn't quite place it.

"I don't know what's wrong with me," the young guy said again.

"There's nothing wrong with you."

Brendan loved how reassuring this Rhys guy was, his voice so warm and kind. What was his young friend so upset about?

"Of course there is. This is, like, the tenth thing I've tried, and none of them worked."

Brendan frowned. Tenth thing? And what did he mean, it didn't work? Unlike what people assumed sometimes, BDSM or kink in its broadest sense was not a cure-all for problems people struggled with. Sure, they could help find release from certain tensions, but it wasn't a fix for everything.

"Raf, it's not been ten. It's been five—I've kept count—and it's not supposed to *work*. It's supposed to tell you if a kink clicks with you or you with the kink. It's supposed to make you feel something, help you find what could be your thing."

Raf. What a cute name for that sweet, young voice. And how glad Brendan was that Raf's companion had such a realistic approach.

"You knew instantly what your thing was," Raf said, and he sounded miserable.

"That's only because I wanted to be a Dom for all the wrong reasons. I thought it would impress Cornell. It so happened I was actually good at it and really connected with it. But I'm still discovering stuff I like and dislike in training with Ford."

Ah, he was Ford's protégé. Brendan could picture him now, the Rhys he'd met briefly a few weeks ago when Ford had approached him if his mentee could watch Brendan administer a spanking. Rhys was young, twenty-one or so, if Brendan remembered correctly. But he'd been polite, eager to learn, and he'd taken it seriously. No wonder with Ford as a mentor. That man didn't take on just anyone.

"I know," Raf said, sounding even sadder than before. "I'm angry with myself and so disappointed. I really thought I'd connect with puppy play, you know? But it made me feel stupid and not happy and free at all. That Dom was hella annoyed with me as well."

"You *were* kind of disobedient," Rhys said, and for the first time, his voice took on a slight edge. "If you'd been my sub, I would've paddled your ass red for that, just so you know."

"I know," Raf said, and Brendan had to strain his ears to hear him, his voice was so small. "I'm sorry. I'm not good at obeying."

"You can be, though," Rhys said. "That's what frustrates

me sometimes. I know you like being told what to do when I do it, and I can't figure out why you can't do it in a scene."

"I don't know either," Raf said, and Brendan could hear the tears in his voice. "But a few sessions more like this one, and no Dom will want to play with me anymore."

Brendan's heart filled with compassion at the heartbreak in that simple statement. He'd seen it before—boys who struggled to fit in, even in a community made up of what most people would consider outliers. If you didn't fit inside the boxes, it wasn't easy to find your place.

"I promise you we'll find where you fit, Raf," Rhys said. "I'm not giving up on you this easily. But can you hang here for half an hour? Master Ford has a demonstration he wants me to watch, and after that, I'll take you home, okay?"

It was quiet for a little bit, but then Raf spoke up again, his voice a bit muffled as if he was being held close, cuddled against Rhys's chest. "Will you make hot cocoa for me when we get home? With marshmallows?"

Brendan jerked upright, his mind on high alert now at that sweet request. Could it be? Was it possible he'd found someone who would appreciate his type of care? It certainly had the potential of being exactly what this boy needed.

"Of course. Hang tight, okay? I'll be back as soon as I can."

"Okay."

"And Raf, please don't wander off. It makes it hard for me to find you, and you could get into trouble, remember?"

"Right. I remember. I'll wait here, Rhys."

There was some rustling, and then Rhys walked by. Brendan wasn't sure why, but he listened in hard, anticipating what started mere seconds after Rhys had left his friend alone.

The sound of a boy crying.

RAF TRIED to keep it quiet. The last thing he wanted was to become a bother to someone else tonight. His father used to say Raf had filled his quota of stupidity for that week, and that's how he felt tonight, like he'd more than filled his quota for being a bother. God, Rhys had to be sick and tired of him by now. The thought of losing his best friend made his heart hurt even more.

He tried to keep his sobs in, but he couldn't hold them back, the sadness too overwhelming to be kept inside. He was such a failure. At everything. At twenty-two, he had no job despite the college degree he'd worked so hard to get, no boyfriend, a crappy apartment he shared with a total asshole who stole his food half the time, and no fucking clue about how to be an adult. Life sucked, and he kept hoping things would get better, but they didn't.

And now this, another failure at discovering where he fit in. He'd tried doing what Rhys had told him, to simply obey the Dom and not worry about anything else. But his mind didn't work that way. The puppy gear had been cute at first, and he'd liked being able to play, but then the Dom had given commands like *fetch*, and Raf had gone in his head.

Was he supposed to walk or crawl? Bark? Could he use his hands? Why did the other puppies have a tail and he didn't? Oh, he wanted a long one like that big, furry pup. That had to feel good in your ass. Would it rub against your pleasure spot when you moved? He bet it did. And before he knew it, he'd stopped listening and had one highly irritated Dom on his hands.

Why could his brain never cooperate and focus for once? The fact that he'd had a hard time lately sticking to the schedule for his meds didn't help either. In high school and the first year of college, it had been easier because Rhys had helped him set alarms on his phone. But then he'd dropped his phone in the toilet—and it had drowned, of course—and he'd bought a new one, and he'd forgotten to put the alarms back on. Adulting was hard, and he sucked at it.

Surrendering to the intense sense of hopelessness inside him, Raf put his hands on the table and buried his head in them, wishing he could stop thinking for just five minutes. Stop thinking, stop worrying, stop jumping from thought to thought without ever having peace. Just *stop*.

"Can I join you?" a warm, male voice asked, and Raf's head shot up.

The man standing at his booth was utter perfection. He had to be in his forties, with silver hairs between his brown hair and in his short beard. He was wearing a simple black T-shirt that showed off his big arms and chest, his chest hair peeping from the V-neck. Raf's gaze dropped lower to a soft, slightly round belly and a pair of thick thighs in simple jeans. He was the epitome of a silver bear, and Raf's mouth watered.

When the man kept holding his gaze, Raf realized he'd been asked a question...and that he was a blubbering mess while this man was sheer perfection. God, the timing couldn't have been worse. Why couldn't this guy have seen him two hours before, when he'd been happy and cute as fuck?

Oh, he still hadn't answered his question, though the man showed no signs of impatience yet. "I'm not at my best right now," Raf said.

The man smiled. "That wasn't the question," he said. "It was a simple yes or no."

Huh. He had a point. "Yes?" Raf said hesitantly, not sure why the man would want to sit with him.

The man scooted into the booth, finding a spot so close to Raf he could smell the woody scent of his cologne. "I'm Daddy Brendan, but you can call me Brendan for now."

Somehow, Raf's mind got stuck on those last words. "For now?"

Brendan's smile widened. "One step at a time, boy. You're Raf, am I right?"

How did he know that? Oh god, had he heard about him yet from other Doms? Had he fucked things up so badly Doms were already gossiping about him behind his back? Tears pushed behind his eyes all over again.

"Look at me, boy," Brendan said, and Raf looked. There was something in Brendan's voice that made him want to. "All you have to do is answer my question, nothing else."

Okay. He could do that. "Yes, I'm Raf. How did you know?"

"I overheard you talking with your friend," Brendan said, and Raf wanted to *die* right fucking now.

"That was a private conversation," he offered weakly.

Brendan shook his head. "Not at that volume in a club like this, it's not."

"You're not even gonna apologize for listening in?" Raf said, intimidated and indignant at the same time.

"Nope, because I may be able to help you."

"Help me?" Raf asked, intrigued now. "With what?"

"With finding where you fit in, what kink would work for you."

Raf brought his hand to his nose to wipe it off, but Brendan grabbed his wrist. "Not with your hand," he said, his voice mild but with that little edge to it that made Raf pay attention. Brendan took a cocktail napkin from the little holder on the table. "Use this."

Brendan released his wrist, and Raf took the napkin, then wiped his nose. Brendan handed him another one. "Blow your nose," he instructed.

Blow your nose? What was he, five? Still, Raf did as he was told, then crumpled up the napkins and stuffed them into his pockets. No way was he leaving those on the table. That was just gross.

To his surprise, Brendan took another napkin, then turned to him and asked, "Can I touch you?"

Raf nodded, too curious to even speak.

"Use your words, boy."

"Yes," Raf said immediately. "What were you...?"

He couldn't even finish his sentence because Brendan reached for him with the napkin, dabbing his eyes and drying his tears. It was a move so sweet and unexpected that Raf almost started crying again. Who and what was this man?

"Tell me what you've tried so far." It wasn't even a question.

Raf debated whether he wanted to share his humiliation with this perfect stranger. Then again, what use was it to hold back now? If the man had overheard him talking to Rhys, he already got the gist of it anyway.

"I started with ropes because Rhys thought it might help me become quiet in my head. Master Ford tied me up so I could feel if that would help me calm down. It didn't. He ended it before I could use my safe word. But he was really nice about it and said it wasn't for everyone, that a lot of people had trouble sitting still."

Brendan nodded. "Very true. It's definitely not my thing, not as a Dom either."

Encouraged by that, Raf tried to remember what the second thing had been. The puppy play had been today, but what else had he done? Oh, right, the blindfolding disaster. He sighed. "Turns out that when you blindfold me, I get very angsty about not being able to see what's happening, and my brain won't stop worrying. Or talking."

He peeked at Brendan from underneath his eyelashes, but the man never laughed at him. "Okay. So you found out that doesn't work either."

"Neither does pain." Raf felt emboldened by the man's reactions so far. "We tried that in two different sessions, and it doesn't do anything for me, except hurt. I see these sessions where people are being flogged and whipped, and they fucking love it, but I just wince when I see that."

"No cuss words," Brendan said.

Raf frowned. What now?

"When you're with me, I don't want to hear cuss words coming out of your mouth. You didn't know, so I'll let this one pass, but from now on, no cuss words."

Raf opened his mouth to ask if the man was fucking kidding, but one look at his face made him reconsider. Okay, then. That would take some getting used to.

"I'll try." He wanted to show his good intentions.

"I'll make sure to give you proper incentives and deterrents," Brendan said rather cryptically. "But please continue."

What were they talking about again? Oh, right, his failures. Raf sighed again. "I assume you heard about today's unmitigated disaster with the puppy thing?"

"From what I understood, that failed to grab your interest as well." Raf thought that was the politest way of describing it ever.

"That was it. Oh, wait, I forgot about the kneeling

session. That was…" He waved his hands, searching for a way to put it into words. "The Dom kept calling me a brat, and it took me a while to figure out he didn't mean it as a compliment." His shoulders dropped. "I suck at this. What am I doing wrong? I don't understand. Maybe it's my brain."

He clasped his hands together, then popped his knuckles because it was such a satisfying sound. Brendan put a big, strong hand on his, squeezing gently but with enough pressure to get his attention, and Raf stopped.

"You're doing nothing wrong, boy."

Raf decided he liked the way Brendan said that word. *Boy*. He was far from the first person to use that term, but it sounded different coming from him. More intense, somehow. As if he meant it.

"Raf, I want to try something with you, if you're open to it," Brendan said, still holding Raf's hands.

Raf looked up, not sure what this perfect man could possibly want to try with him. "You don't need to take pity on me," he said softly. "I appreciate it, but I'm not your problem."

"Honey, you're no one's *problem*. You should be someone's precious boy, but never a problem."

Raf let out a small sigh. "That's really sweet of you to say. I doubt anyone would agree with you, but it's nice to hear."

"I'm a patient man, so we have time. But I'll need your permission to try, boy. What do you say? Are you willing to trust one more time?"

2

Brendan almost held his breath, waiting for the adorable boy to agree. God, he hoped he'd gotten through to him enough to make him curious, to make him want to try. The boy had been hurt and rejected, that was clear, and oh, Brendan's heart *ached* for him. He couldn't bear it, those big blue eyes that radiated so much pain.

Raf bit his lip, studying Brendan. "What are you going to do?"

Brendan smiled. "Nothing you don't want, I promise. All you'd have to do is say stop, and we'll stop instantly."

"I thought *stop* wasn't considered a good safe word."

"It's not, but you don't need a safe word for what we're doing. This is not a scene, Raf, merely something I want to try. Do you trust me?"

Raf kept worrying that full bottom lip, and Brendan made a mental note to discourage him from that habit. He had other uses in mind for those perfect lips.

"I can't go anywhere," the boy said. "I promised Rhys I would stay here."

"And do you usually do what Rhys tells you to?" Brendan was curious about the relationship between those two because it sounded like it wasn't a standard friendship.

Raf's cheeks grew a little red. "Not always, but I try to. He's really smart, and he always looks out for me. Plus, when I don't listen and I get into trouble, he gets this look and tone that I don't like," Raf confessed.

Brendan kept his face carefully blank, but inside, he was elated with the answers and clues Raf was sharing. It almost seemed too good to be true, which was why his little experiment was so important. The last thing he wanted was another Henry on his hands.

"Hmm, I see. And you don't like it when he gets that tone with you?"

Raf shook his head vehemently at first, but then he hesitated. "No, but at the same time, I kind of do because it shows that he cares."

There was a story there, Brendan was sure, but not one he would ask for now. They had time. "We'll stay right here in this booth, I promise. When Rhys comes back, he'll find you here, in one piece and out of trouble. What do you say?"

Finally Raf nodded, and Brendan let out an inward sigh of relief. "You'll need to use words, boy," he said.

Raf rumpled his cute button nose. "Why are you Doms always so fucking strict about that? Like, why is that so important?"

Brendan merely lifted an eyebrow at him, making his displeasure obvious. Raf's face fell.

"Oops. Sorry. I didn't mean to cuss."

He looked so contrite that Brendan had no doubt he meant it. "I appreciate you trying. To answer your question, it's all about consent. Consent in this stage has to be verbal so there's no doubt we both agree to this."

Raf nodded, looking serious now. "Okay. I agree to whatever it is you want to do," he said, then frowned. "But it's nothing that will hurt, right? Or that involves, like, bodily fluids? Or sex?"

Brendan chuckled. "Next time, you might want to toss those out there before agreeing," he teased him. "But no, boy. I told you, it's not a scene. I need permission to touch you and your promise you'll try to do what I ask you."

Worry instantly clouded Raf's face. "I'm not very good at following orders," he whispered.

"Let me be the judge of that, okay? You ready to start?"

"Yes," Raf said after a short pause.

"I want you to take your shoes off first."

Raf's face showed curiosity, but he obediently pulled up his feet and untied his colorful sneakers before kicking them off. He met Brendan's eyes with an expectant gaze. "Good boy," Brendan praised him, watching with amazement as Raf's face lit up like fireworks. God, he was *starving* for it, and he had no idea.

Brendan dropped his gaze to the tight jeans the boy was wearing that appeared like he'd need help to peel them off. He had to admit they looked fantastic on him, but they couldn't be comfortable.

"Can you breathe in those?" he asked, pointing at the pants.

Raf smiled as he shrugged. "They're a little tight, but they make my ass pop. I figured it might help me score tonight."

"Take them off, please. I need you to be comfortable. Unless you're not wearing underwear?"

Raf's grin widened. "You bet your ass I am. I'm not putting my junk in these without an extra layer of protection."

Brendan tsked, and Raf's smile vanished. "Sorry for cussing," he said, his shoulders dropping a little.

"I'm not upset with you, Raf. You're trying really hard, and that's all that matters."

Some of the tension left Raf, and he leaned back in the booth, stretching his legs. Then he started shimmying out of his pants. Brendan watched, his eyes glued to the spectacle of that lean, graceful body maneuvering itself to get out of those impossible jeans. The waistband of his boxer briefs rode dangerously low as he pulled it down, revealing nothing but smooth skin. He shaved or waxed, and Brendan's cock was throbbing at the thought. Such a perfect boy, and Raf didn't even realize it.

It took Raf a little while, but he managed to get rid of his jeans, dumping them in a crumpled heap on the seat. He looked at Brendan, and the expectancy in his eyes was easy to spot.

"Thank you," Brendan said. "You're such a good boy for me."

Raf *beamed*. There was no other word for it, his whole face lighting up and his shoulders straightening.

"I'd love for you to come sit on my lap," Brendan said, wording it so Raf could easily refuse. But apparently, the praise was addictive enough for the boy to overcome any reservations he still had, and he slid onto Brendan's lap in a second, parking himself there as if he belonged there. And he did, Brendan thought, but the boy just didn't know it yet.

Raf shifted a little, his bottom encountering Brendan's hard cock, trapped inside his jeans. "You're hard," Raf said, his voice filled with wonder.

Brendan smiled at him. "You're a sexy boy, Raf."

Raf cocked his head. "You feel like you're big."

A laugh erupted from Brendan's lips. "I am, compared to the average anyway."

"Mmm." Raf licked his lips in a gesture that had Brendan take a deep breath to compose himself.

He pulled Raf against him, folding his arms around him. "Put your head against my chest."

Raf wiggled until he'd found a comfortable position, and Brendan's dick grew only harder. But much more important was the feeling inside him when Raf nestled against him, one arm wrapped around him and his head resting on his chest.

"This is nice," Raf said. "I like cuddling."

"Me too." Brendan's hand slipped under Raf's shirt and found the warm, smooth skin on his back. He stroked him with feather light caresses.

"You have the perfect body to cuddle up against," Raf said, his voice sounding a little dreamy. "It's so big and strong and soft."

Aw, wasn't it nice when his big bear body was properly appreciated? Brendan couldn't compete anymore with the younger Doms, most of whom spent hours training to achieve that whole six-pack look. But he was comfortable being bigger and cuddlier. It fit the type of Dom he was. Plus, as some boys had discovered, his cock made up for a lot. Not that Brendan was interested in boys who only wanted him for a good, hard fuck, but a man had needs, so every now and then he gave in to his urges and used it to his advantage.

"Thank you," he told Raf, who rubbed his cheek against Brendan's shirt.

"You smell good too," the boy said. "Is that cologne you're wearing?"

"Old Spice."

"Yummy. It fits you."

Raf was quiet for a few seconds. "Are we going to do anything else? Not that this isn't nice, but it's not really what I had expected."

"Nope, this is it. We're gonna sit here and cuddle."

"Huh. Okay."

Brendan remembered what the boy had shared so casually earlier, about thinking that maybe his brain was the problem. It seemed he had a hard time shutting it off. Maybe he should help him a little.

"There's one more thing." He held out his thumb to Raf, right in front of his mouth. "Open up, boy."

Raf turned his head, pushing off against his chest, but Brendan pinned him down. "Stay," he said, dropping his voice a little. He pressed his thumb against Raf's lips. "Open up."

He sensed Raf's confusion. "Don't you want me to suck on something else?" the boy said, but his cheeky statement sounded a little forced. He was using sex to create a distraction, Brendan realized.

"Not right now, but I'll keep the offer in mind," he said dryly.

After what seemed like an eternity, Raf opened his mouth, and Brendan pushed his thumb right in. "Suck," he told Raf, who obediently closed his lips around him, sucking Brendan's thumb into his warm, wet mouth. The suction he applied shot straight to Brendan's balls, because of course it did, but he ignored it.

Brendan tightened his other arm around Raf. "Now sit quietly and cuddle with me. That's all you have to do, nothing else. Just let it all go."

Raf fidgeted for the first few minutes, but Brendan didn't give him much leeway, keeping his arms locked around him and pressing Raf against him. Then Brendan felt the tension seeping out of Raf's body, his muscles going soft and relaxed. There was a sigh alongside his thumb, and then Raf sucked for real. Not like you did when sucking cock, but more like a comfort suck, like a lollipop or a binkie. Brendan looked down, and Raf's eyes fluttered before they closed.

He started humming, knowing Raf would be able to hear and feel the vibrations in his chest. Another deep sigh, and then Raf's body relaxed completely. Minutes later, he was asleep.

When Rhys came back, fifteen or so minutes later, Raf was still fully asleep, nestled against Brendan. Rhys came to a sudden stop as he spotted them. "He's *asleep*?" he asked, his face showing his surprise.

Brendan nodded. "He was out like a light fifteen minutes ago," he said softly.

Rhys slid into the booth and sat next to him. "Is he okay?"

"Yeah, he is. He was emotional after you left."

Rhys let out a sigh, rubbing his temples. "I was afraid of that, but I didn't want to blow off Ford either."

"And rightfully so. He's not a man who likes to be kept waiting."

"Thank you. It's nice of you to take care of Raf."

His eyes dropped to Raf again, who still sucked on Brendan's thumb, even in his sleep. Rhys's eyes widened before his face went pensive. "Do you think he'd like being a *little*?"

Brendan was glad Rhys remembered who he was and what his kink was. At least he didn't have to explain that, which could be a frustrating conversation at times. Not everyone got it. Even within the community, his type of Daddy care got the stink eye at times.

"You tell me, Rhys. You know him better than I do," Brendan said, meeting his eyes.

Rhys dragged a hand through his hair, then looked at Raf again. "I thought he might like puppy play. He's as bouncy and restless as a puppy, so I thought it might be a good fit."

Brendan nodded. "I can see that. It still might be, with a Master who knows how to handle him. Something tells me young Raf here needs a lot of structure and discipline but also a lot of affection and praise."

Much to his surprise, Rhys's eyes grew misty. "You have no idea, man. I've wished a thousand times that he and I were compatible, you know? Then I could give him what he needs."

It was touching, the deep friendship between these two. "Rhys, would you be comfortable with me taking him on as my boy? If he wants to, that is."

"You don't need my permission," Rhys said, looking a little puzzled.

"No, but I'd like to have your blessing. It's clear how much you mean to him and he to you."

"You're not talking about a scene here and there," Rhys said, catching on now.

"No. That's not how I roll anyway, but from what I can tell, it's not what Raf needs either. He needs stability...and I've been looking for a boy to take care of."

"Permanently?"

Brendan realized how that might come across to someone their age, but he had to be honest. "Ultimately, yes. I want a boy to call my own, Rhys. Someone I can take care of, who I can play with, discipline, and spoil a little. But we'll need to see if we are as good a match as I think we will be."

"Can I check your references?" Rhys asked, and Brendan's respect for him went up even further.

"Ask Ford. He knows me. Very well, I might add," Brendan said, smiling a little at the memories.

Rhys lifted an eyebrow. "You and Ford? There's a surprising combination. I have a hard time picturing him sitting on your lap and sucking your thumb."

Brendan laughed, keeping it soft as not to wake Raf. "Not my thumb so much, but I have other appendages he was rather fascinated by. Your mentor is vers and a total size whore, didn't you know?"

Rhys's astonished face made him laugh even more, and Raf stirred on his lap. Brendan looked down on him as the boy blinked sleepily, then opened his eyes, turned his head, and gazed up at Brendan. "Hey sweet boy, did you take a little nap?" Brendan asked, unable to resist the urge to press a tender kiss on his forehead.

Raf let go of his thumb, and Brendan pulled it out of his mouth.

"I can't believe I fell asleep," Raf said, sounding a little out of it.

"You needed it. Rhys is here to take you home, so why don't you go with him, hmm?"

Raf looked at him with eyes that were still sleepy but also full of trust and want. "Will I see you again?" he asked rather shyly.

Brendan allowed himself the liberty of kissing those soft, plump lips briefly. "Count on it, my boy."

3

Raf wiped his sweaty hands off on his jeans, then forced himself to ring the doorbell. His heart was racing, and he couldn't stand still, bouncing from one foot to the other. Luckily, he didn't have to wait long. Brendan opened the door, looking all yummy and scrumptious again in a shirt that hugged his broad body and a pair of jeans that showed off his curves and strength.

"Hi," Raf said, feeling self-conscious. He even did a stupid little wave with his hand. How totally lame was that? Ugh. Could he be any more of a spaz?

But Brendan's face broke open in a big smile. "Hey, Raf, come on in."

Rhys had vouched for the man, insisting that it was safe to be at his place. He'd explained that it would actually work better than in the club, but that Brendan would explain it himself to Raf. He couldn't wait because he had questions. About two hundred of them.

"I'm nervous," he told Brendan, then mentally chastised himself for admitting that. His brain was a total squirrel today, running in every direction. And he'd taken his meds because Rhys had texted him to remind him. Twice. It happened some days, his brain going crazy, and especially when he was stressed or nervous. Right now, he was both.

A strong hand landed on his shoulder, and his head jerked up. He'd been staring at the floor without seeing anything, the flurry of thoughts in his head too distracting. "It's okay, Raf," Brendan said in that calm voice, and Raf believed him.

He blew out a breath. "Sorry."

Brendan moved his hand from his shoulder to Raf's chin, forcing him to meet his eyes. "We'll talk about the rules in a little bit, but here's the first one. Don't say sorry unless you broke one of my rules. Being nervous is not a reason to say sorry."

"How about being major awkward and a total klutz? Does that count? Or saying stupid shit because your filter isn't working?" Brendan's eyes narrowed a bit, and Raf realized what he had said. "That's something I *am* supposed to say sorry for, right? The cussing?"

Brendan nodded.

"Sorry. I didn't mean to."

"I know," Brendan said, the smile back in his eyes, and Raf sighed with relief.

Brendan let go of his chin, then stepped back. "You can take your shoes off and put them in your cubby by the door."

Raf kicked off his sneakers. Various hooks were screwed into the wall, each at a different height. Underneath was a bench that had squares with storage space for shoes in them. When he bent over, he discovered one with his name on it.

"I have a cubby?" he asked, completely flabbergasted.

"Yes," Brendan simply said, not offering more.

Huh, how about that? Raf put his shoes in the cubby, then hung his jacket on the hook above it. It looked neat. He could see why Brendan liked it.

"Thank you," Brendan said in that warm tone of his that made Raf feel so good inside. "Would you like apple juice or red fruit juice to drink?"

"I'm not supposed to have the red juice. I react to the food coloring and get even more hyper."

"We can double-check, but I think the one I have should be safe, since it has no artificial coloring and only uses natural ingredients."

Much to Raf's surprise, Brendan was right. Even more surprising, he didn't offer the juice in a glass but in a plastic cup, one of those cups Raf knew from when he'd been little. It was a funny choice, but he kinda liked it. The blue color was so vivid.

"Let's go sit in the living room for a bit and chat." Brendan walked into the living room, and Raf followed him.

God, the place was organized. It was a far cry from the utter mess his own room was in, and he cringed at the thought Brendan would see it. He'd have to do some serious cleaning if he ever invited him over. But maybe he was way ahead of things, as usual. After all, they were supposed to talk today. That's what Brendan had said when he'd called Raf to set up today's date. Wait, was it even a date? He was flying blind here.

"Raf," Brendan said, and his voice alone was enough to bring Raf out of his thoughts. "Why don't you come sit on the couch next to me?"

Raf eagerly found a spot, crossing his legs and turning sideways so he could see Brendan. "Your house is so tidy." He bit his lip. "Don't ever come by unannounced at my place. It's a pigsty."

Brendan gave him a friendly smile. "I promise I won't. You'll find there's very little I do unannounced or unplanned."

Wow. That was something he'd never even considered: there were people who actually *planned* things. His mind wanted to latch on to that thought and worry about him and Brendan being complete opposites, but Raf pushed it down. For once, his brain cooperated.

"Can you tell me a little about yourself and what you're looking for?" Brendan asked.

Raf sat up straight. This was a question he'd been expecting, and he was prepared. "I'm twenty-two, and I finished my degree in early childhood education a few months ago. I'm hoping to get a job at a pre-K or kindergarten as a teacher's aide. I love kids," he added, smiling. "They're so pure and honest, and they still know how to have fun."

"I love kids as well."

Raf sighed with relief that they at least had that in common. "As for what I'm looking for..." His face pulled tight. "I wish I knew. A connection, that's what I'm looking for. With something, with someone, I don't know."

"A relationship?"

Raf nodded. "Sure. I hook up as well, but I don't really like it. It's too complicated."

Brendan cocked his head, looking at him with interest. "Most people would say relationships are more complicated than hookups."

"True, but I'm not most people. My brain works differently, and hookups make me anxious. So do relationships, come to think of it, so maybe I don't know what the hell I'm talking about."

It didn't seem to bother Brendan, his ramblings and his revelations so far, which made Raf relax.

"Sex?"

Raf shrugged. "I like a good fuck as much as the next person, but half the time, I can't be bothered. It's so much effort for so little in return. I mean, if I want a good orgasm, I can fuck myself with a toy. I don't need a guy for that, and it's far less messy."

"Do you like things ordered and neat?"

Raf thought that was a funny question to ask. Also, Brendan didn't seem to object to Raf using crude words in this context.

"I never seem to manage it, but yeah. The psychologist who diagnosed me said it would help to create outward order so as to calm the chaos inside me. Or something like that. It sounds a hell of a lot easier in theory than in reality," Raf said, sighing. "I seem to create order and chaos wherever I go. It's not what I want, but it's how I'm wired, I guess."

"Hmm," Brendan said, but there was no judgment in his voice or on his face. "Anything else you wanna tell me?"

"Safe sex only, I'm an exclusive bottom, and my safe word is pineapple."

"*Pineapple?* Boy, you've been watching way too much gay porn," Brendan said, but he was laughing, that big body of his shaking with it.

Raf smiled back. "I've been single for a long time."

He wasn't gonna apologize for watching porn, but Brendan didn't look like he expected him to, which was interesting. Apparently, saying "fuck" or "shit" was something to apologize for, but admitting to watching gay porn and talking about sex wasn't.

Then Brendan's face sobered. "Raf, do you know what kind of Dom I am?"

Raf nodded, his face showing the eagerness of someone who knew the correct answer. "You're a Daddy-Dom. You told me when we met, remember? Daddy Brendan, you said."

Something flashed over Brendan's face, but it was gone too fast for Raf to make anything of it. "Yes, but I'm a special Daddy."

"Oh?" Raf leaned forward with his elbows resting on his knees.

There was more than one type of Daddy? Raf had thought it was one category: the type of Dom who was softer and more caring. Rhys had suggested it was something that might fit Raf. Raf hadn't said anything, but he'd figured the last thing he'd need was another Daddy. His real dad was enough of an asshole to cure him of the desire for a father figure.

But maybe Daddy Brendan could dissuade him of that notion. With a body like that, the man had some serious convincing points already. Plus, he'd been super nice and caring so far, and Raf *liked* it when he told him what to do because he was so kind when he did it.

"I'm a Daddy who loves his boys to be what's called a 'little.' Age play, as it's also referred to. It means a boy sinks into a different persona where he's little again."

Oh. Raf's mind caught on quickly. He'd read about this, or maybe Rhys had told him once, back when he'd explained all the different types of kink there were. On one hand, he'd been fascinated by it, but on the other hand, it had seemed weird to him. Wearing diapers again, drinking from sippy cups, there was little *sexy* about that. Then again, the idea of being taken care of did appeal to him, and he'd seen a picture of a Daddy playing with his little with some toys, and that had made Raf a little jealous.

"I can tell by your face you've come across this."

Raf nodded. "I have questions and stuff, but I'm interested."

"You are?"

For the first time, Raf became aware the man had feared rejection. He thought of the way Brendan had taken care of him in the club a few days ago, the way he'd held Raf and had him suck on his thumb. That made a whole lot more sense now as well, and man, he'd never felt as safe and protected in his life. Enough to fall asleep on the lap of a stranger in the middle of a club.

"Yeah," Raf said softly. "Very much so."

RELIEF FLOODED BRENDAN'S INSIDES. Things were going well. Far better, in fact, than he had dared hope.

"That makes me very happy," he said, sending Raf a broad smile, which he returned instantly.

The boy was so beautiful when he smiled, his whole face lighting up. He was gorgeous anyway, but he had worry lines too often, little marks of stress on his forehead and on the bridge of his nose.

"But I don't know what to do," Raf said, his smile already faltering. "I've never done this before. Not that that's saying much because there's a lot I've never tried, but I don't want to disappoint you."

Brendan began to see how insecure he was. He wasn't sure what had happened to Raf, but clearly, someone had damaged his self-confidence and his ability to trust people. Brendan's money was on one or both of his parents, since that was often the case, sadly.

"That's the easiest part of being a little," Brendan said,

his voice warm and affirming. "You don't have to do anything, except what I tell you. I promise I will tell you exactly what I expect of you, okay? Clear rules, clear punishment."

"P-punishment?" Raf's eyes widened.

Brendan nodded. "Yes, because naughty boys should get punished, don't you think?"

Raf looked puzzled. "When you say it like that, with your voice all low and sexy, it doesn't sound like punishment."

Brendan couldn't hold back his smile. "Some punishments you'll find as much pleasure as annoyance, but I promise you that I also can come up with things you really won't like."

Raf grinned, his tension gone now. "I bet you can. You look like a strict Daddy to me."

"I am, but I will also spoil you to pieces, baby boy."

Raf let out a little sigh. "I think I'll like that part. So how do we start?"

As much as Brendan wanted to jump into things, they hadn't discussed everything they needed to yet. "You mentioned sex briefly, but that's something we need to talk about a little more. Is that something you wanna take slow, or how do you feel about it?"

Raf shrugged. "I don't need to go slow. I mean, if we're not compatible on the Daddy thing, at least we can both get a good fuck out of it."

Brendan couldn't put his finger on why that casual statement hurt him. Not for himself, but for Raf. "You're worth a lot more than a good fuck, Raf. I hope you know that."

Another shrug, though his eyes sparked with something Brendan couldn't define. "We'll see," was his noncommittal answer—an answer Brendan didn't like at all. He let it go for now, but this was definitely something he needed to think about.

"How about we experiment a little?" he asked. "Just to see if you connect with it."

Raf nodded, the hint of pain that had been on his face before gone. "Yes, please."

"Okay, here are the rules. You can call me Brendan for now. You don't have to say 'sir,' but you can say 'Daddy,' but only if you feel like it. If it feels forced, let it go."

Raf nodded again, a serious expression on his face.

"Let's play for an hour. In that hour, you only have to do what I tell you. There's nothing else for you to worry about, okay? Be yourself and do what comes natural."

Another serious nod, Raf's nose crumpling in concentration.

"We're not gonna do anything sexual. I want to make that clear to manage expectations. This hour is to see if it clicks for you, okay?"

"Can I ask something?"

"Sure."

"If we're not gonna do anything sexual, then what *are* we going to do?"

Brendan smiled at him. "We're gonna play." He got up from the couch and extended his hand to Raf. "Are you coming with me, baby boy?"

Raf hesitated for maybe two seconds before he accepted his hand and allowed himself to be pulled up from the couch.

"If we're gonna play, you need to wear something more comfortable than those jeans, no matter how sexy they are. I have something for you I hope you'll love."

He'd estimated Raf's size, but now that he looked at him again, he was pretty sure he'd gotten it right. They walked up to the special playroom Brendan had built and furnished with so much care, hoping that one day, he'd have a boy to spoil and care for in there. After Henry, he'd feared he'd never be able to trust again, yet here he was, feeling hopeful for the first time in a long time.

Brendan pulled Raf gently into the room, watching him as he took it all in. The room held a full-size daybed with comfy pillows and a superheroes comforter. Along one wall, a low cabinet contained several bins of toys, with a large play rug in front of it with streets, train tracks, and even an airport printed on it—perfect to play on with toy cars. In the corner stood a rocking chair, Brendan's favorite place to sit with a boy on his lap.

The changing table was handcrafted for him by a local guy who was brilliant with woodwork. He'd built it at the perfect height so Brendan wouldn't have to bend over, and even attached a pair of stairs so the boy could climb on himself. On that changing table lay the outfit Brendan had picked out for Raf: a short-sleeved dark blue onesie with cute little monkeys holding bananas.

Raf let out an audible gasp as he looked around the room. "This is..." He seemed to search for words. "This is really special. It's a happy room."

Brendan smiled, deeply satisfied with that answer. "It is." He pulled Raf over to the changing table. "How about you put on some comfy play clothes?" He pointed at the onesie.

Raf's eyes widened. "I can wear that?"

"I bought it especially for you. The monkeys reminded me of you. Mischievous and full of energy."

Raf chuckled but then quieted as he looked at the changing table. "Do you want me to wear a diaper?"

Brendan gently tugged at his hand until Raf faced him. "Not today. I would love for you to try it at some point, but I would never pressure you. We have time, baby boy. We can take things slow."

"I'm not good at slow."

Brendan pressed a kiss on his head. "That's okay because you don't set the pace here. I do, baby boy. So, what do you say? Wanna change into something more comfortable?"

Raf stared at the onesie, his face showing he was thinking hard about something. "I'd like that."

Brendan wanted to cheer. The first victory was in the bag. "Do you want to do it yourself, or would you like Daddy to help you?"

Raf's teeth went into his bottom lip, and he kept staring at the onesie for a long time. "That's what you like, isn't it? To do things like that for me and with me."

"Very much. The more you let me do for you, the happier I'll be. I want to take care of you, baby boy, as much as you'll let me." Brendan saw no need to be secretive about his desires.

"Okay. I want to try that."

Brendan's heart burst with joy, and his face broke open in a big smile. "You're such a good boy for Daddy," he said, watching Raf's face light up at that praise. "Raise your arms for me so I can take your shirt off."

Raf obeyed instantly. Brendan pulled his shirt off, folding it quickly and putting it on the dressing table. Then he kneeled in front of Raf and reached for his jeans.

"Pants are next," he said, thinking it best to communicate his intentions clearly. Raf looked down on him as Brendan took his jeans off as well, leaving him in a pair of pale pink, tight, sexy boxer briefs. They showed Raf's cock had taken an interest and was half-hard, which was a reassurance to Brendan.

"I'm not very big," Raf said, his tone apologetic.

"You're perfect. Absolutely perfect and exquisite."

He helped Raf into the onesie, holding it up as the boy stepped in, then buttoned it up for him. The blue color was perfect on him, making his eyes pop, and Brendan had gotten the size right. It would look even better with a plump diapered bottom, but he had patience.

"You look adorable," he told Raf as he rose to his feet, his voice a little emotional to his own surprise.

Raf looked at himself, then smiled. "I love it."

"Good. Now, let's play. We have plenty of toys for you to play with, but today, I thought it would be fun if we built a train track. What do you say?"

Raf stared at him as if he'd spoken a foreign language. "A train track?"

Brendan walked over to the big bin with the wooden train tracks and pulled it out. "Look, we can build a huge track with these, see that?" He pulled open the other bin, which contained all the trains and carriages he had. "And we can make several trains here. There's even little houses you can put along the track."

Raf's face showed pure stress. "I don't understand what you want me to do."

Brendan hurried over to him and put his hands on Raf's shoulders. "I want you to play with trains, baby boy. That's all you have to do, nothing else."

"But what's in it for you? I don't get how this can be rewarding for you."

His little boy was a worrywart. Or maybe this, too, tied back to the deep fear of disappointing someone that Brendan had spotted before. "That's not something you ever have to worry about, Raf. I appreciate your concern, but that's not your job, you know? But I'll answer this time to help you understand. Seeing you happy, that's my reward. I get deep satisfaction out of taking care of you and making sure you're happy and carefree. That's all I want."

Raf worried his bottom lip, his eyes seeking Brendan's. "So if I play with the trains and do nothing else, that's enough to make you happy?"

"If playing with the trains makes you happy, then that's enough for me," Brendan nuanced it a little.

"Huh," Raf said, his voice filled with surprise. "Okay."

"Do you like trains?" Brendan asked, wanting to make sure that wasn't the issue.

Raf smiled instantly. "Yeah. I played with my train track for hours when I was a kid. My dad made me put them in storage when I was ten, saying I was too old for them, but I loved them."

Brendan extended his hand to him. "Then let's play, baby boy."

They found a spot on the soft rug, Brendan sitting down right next to Raf, who emptied out both bins and started building right away. The first few minutes, Brendan helped him by giving suggestions and handing him pieces, but then Raf took over himself. With the tip of his tongue peeping from between his lips, he built a track throughout half the room, even looping under the legs of the changing table. Brendan pulled back a little, finding a spot where he could lean with his back against the wall, and watched Raf play, his heart exploding with joy.

4

Raf hadn't even noticed Brendan had left the room until he came back and lowered himself onto the floor, holding out the cup with his juice. "You need to drink a little, baby boy."

Raf sat up and took the cup, drinking it greedily. He'd been thirsty and hadn't even realized it, too caught up in his play.

Brendan smiled as he took the cup back, then held out a little plastic bowl with apple slices. Something clicked inside Raf, something deep and profound. He looked at the train track, then at the clock on the wall, which told him almost an hour and a half had passed. He'd been completely lost in playing, his head quiet and happy, his body more relaxed than it'd been in ages.

He'd found it. He'd found what he'd been looking for. If he could have this peace with Brendan, this silence in his head, he'd do anything for him.

His eyes teared up, and he blindly reached for the bowl with the apple slices. "Thank you, Daddy," he said, but then that didn't seem enough, and on impulse, he crawled over to him and settled on his lap.

Daddy Brendan took the bowl from him and put it down on the floor, then circled those strong arms around him and held him tight. "What's wrong, my baby boy?"

Raf fought against the tears, not wanting to lose it, but he couldn't hold them back. "I've found it," he choked out on a cry. "You gave me what I was looking for, what I needed."

"Oh, my sweet boy," Daddy Brendan said, his arms tightening around him. "My sweet, precious boy."

Raf's body shook from his sobs now, a sadness releasing from a place inside him that had felt too imprisoned for too long. "Thank you," he said, his voice barely audible as he buried his face against Brendan's strong shoulder. "Thank you, Daddy."

His father had always berated him when he cried, spouting all that crap about manning up and not wanting to appear a sissy. But Daddy Brendan merely held him, whispering sweet words in his hair, making him feel safe. They sat as Raf cried his heart out, letting go of pain he'd never realized he'd been holding in.

When his sobs quieted down, he felt exhausted. He rubbed his wet cheek against Daddy Brendan's T-shirt, then found a perfect spot to put his head and closed his eyes.

"Baby boy, is there anywhere you need to be today?" Daddy Brendan whispered.

Raf tried to think. Did he have any appointments? Rhys had said he'd stop by to chat about how things had gone with Daddy Brendan. "Rhys," he said, too tired to provide more details.

"Come on, sweet boy, let's put you in bed."

Raf's eyes filled with tears all over again as Daddy

Brendan managed to stand up holding him, then walked him over to the bed and gently laid him down. The bed was fluffy and smelled like freshly washed linens, like the dryer sheets Rhys's mom had always used. Raf smiled as Daddy Brendan tucked him in.

Warm lips pressed against his, Daddy's beard tickling his skin. "Sleep well, my precious boy. Daddy will be here when you wake up."

Raf closed his eyes and surrendered, falling asleep instantly.

He woke up disoriented, though feeling safe and snuggly. When he opened his eyes, he immediately found Daddy Brendan sitting in the rocking chair, reading a book. His eyes still swollen from his crying fit, Raf pushed back a new round of tears at the realization that Daddy Brendan had kept his promise.

His father had made so many promises to him as a kid—and he'd kept precious few of them. Even the small ones, like being present at a baseball game—the sport he'd only played because his father had loved it so much—or coming to a school performance, he'd so often canceled. He'd always had valid reasons, or so he'd claimed. Work, mostly. But in the end, Raf had gotten the message, and he'd stopped asking. Stopped trusting too, as he'd learned promises meant little.

And yet here he sat, Daddy Brendan, exactly as he promised. Raf's heart ached with want. "Daddy," he whispered, and Daddy Brendan looked up from his book instantly, his mouth pulling up in a smile.

"Hey, baby boy, did you have a nice nap?"

Raf yawned, stretching his body. "I was super tired." He looked at the clock. Holy crap, he'd slept for two hours. "I need to text Rhys," he said, fully awake now.

Daddy Brendan had gotten up and now kneeled beside him. "I already did. He knows you're still here. He said to text him whenever you're ready to leave."

"Oh," Raf said, sagging back onto the bed. "That's good. Thank you. I hate worrying him."

Daddy Brendan's hand found his hair, rubbing gently. "He's a good friend to you. I'm so happy you have him, but he's lucky to have you as well."

Raf turned on his side and faced him. "I guess things didn't really go as planned today."

Daddy Brendan smiled. "They went better than planned, wouldn't you say? I loved watching you play with the tracks, and I'm so happy you got a good nap in."

"I haven't been sleeping well lately."

"How come?"

Raf hesitated only briefly but then decided to take the jump and trust him. "I have ADHD. Do you know what that is?"

He'd learned not to assume people knew what it was, since some people only had a rudimentary idea or had a lot of wrong opinions.

Brendan frowned a little, but not in a bad way, more like he was thinking. "I have a general idea, but what does it mean for you?"

"It's a lot of different things, but it means my brain is very busy. Trouble concentrating, issues with remembering what I've read, a total squirrel brain, and that's just the beginning. I forget to do a lot of things, and that's very annoying, apparently," he added, feeling more miserable with each symptom he listed. "Then there's the fact that it's hard for me to start something...or to finish it, and I'm a huge slob, even though my brain does better with structure.

It's..." He sighed deeply, avoiding Daddy Brendan's eyes now out of fear of what he'd see there. "It's hard."

He clearly hadn't thought this through, dumping this all on the man at once. And that after the lovely afternoon they'd had. Damn his impulsive brain all over again.

"I can imagine," Brendan said. "It explains some things I noticed in you. I'm sorry it's been a struggle for you. Is that also why you've had trouble sleeping?"

Raf swallowed. So far Daddy Brendan seemed to take it well. Better than he could've hoped for anyway. "That's because I need to take my meds in the morning, and I often forget. When I take them too late in the day, they keep me up at night, and I don't fall asleep till two or three in the morning."

"Hmm. Maybe we should find a way to make sure you don't forget to take them then."

Raf swallowed again. "*We*?" he asked, his voice croaking a little.

"Yes, we," Daddy Brendan said, his voice firm but warm. "It's my job to take care of you, baby boy, so this will fall under my tasks. We'll figure out how we can best do this."

Raf's heart filled with something he hadn't felt in a long time.

Hope.

TWO DAYS LATER, Brendan was still on cloud nine with how well the first experiment with Raf had gone over. The boy had taken to it like a fish to water, and Brendan hoped for much more than he probably should. It was still only the beginning, and a lot could happen, but oh, how Brendan longed and wanted.

He tried to warn himself he shouldn't get his hopes up too high, not after the way Henry had broken things off, leaving Brendan hurting deeply, but it was useless. Raf was everything he'd wanted, all he could've wished for in a boy. Brendan knew the boy was new to this, so he'd have to go slow, but he couldn't help dreaming big.

He'd called Raf the next day at ten in the morning. The boy was supposed to have messaged him as soon as he was awake, but when that didn't happen, Brendan suspected he'd forgotten. Turned out he'd been right. Raf had apologized profusely, but he'd gotten distracted by a job ad he'd spotted online.

Brendan didn't like it, but he'd done a little research on ADHD in the meantime, and he'd learned a lot. Forgetting things was quite common, as was getting distracted. It wasn't something Raf chose; it happened to him, his brain unable to focus or stay on track. So Brendan would adapt and try to understand. The fact that Raf had clearly felt bad had helped.

The next day, Raf *had* remembered to call him when he woke up, and Brendan had seen that as a victory. He'd reminded him to take his meds, which made Raf strangely emotional. The boy soaked up the care and attention like a dying plant soaked up water and sunlight.

Raf didn't have much to do during the day, except scour the Internet for jobs and work an occasional shift at Target, and so Brendan decided he could afford to take a Wednesday afternoon off and spend it with his boy. Waiting till the weekend seemed way too long, and a mere hour or two in the evening were nowhere near enough. So he'd asked Raf to come over again, and he'd planned something he hoped the boy would love… and that would maybe take them to the next step.

Raf showed up ten minutes late, but he had a good reason. "I got invited for a job interview!" he exclaimed as soon as Brendan opened the door for him.

Brendan barely had time to brace himself before he had his arms full of a bumbling, happy Raf. Brendan breathed him in, his soul quieting, now that his boy was close to him again. "I'm so excited for you. I knew you could do it."

"It's for a teacher's aide job at the kindergarten in the elementary school three blocks from here," Raf said as he let go, his eyes sparkling. "It would be perfect for me, and I have the qualifications for it."

"I'm sure you'll do well in the interview."

He got Raf some juice, and they went into the living room, where Raf clearly had trouble sitting still. His foot tapping and his fingers fidgeting, he was almost bouncing in his seat. "Sorry. I'm super excited. I really need a job, you know? It's getting tight financially, and I don't wanna have to move back in with my mom. I'm working some shifts at Target, running the register or restocking, but it's not what I wanna do with my life. Hey, I don't even know what you do for a living? Do you work? I assume you do 'cause you have such a nice house, but what do you do?"

Wow, he *was* hyper. "Come here," Brendan told Raf. He needed to help him calm down a bit. Good thing he'd gotten something at the store that might help. He dragged it out of his pocket, hiding it from Raf for now. "Come sit on my lap for a bit."

To his credit, Raf instantly got up, but before he could climb onto Brendan's lap, he held Raf back with a hand against his chest. "You're wearing those ridiculously tight pants again," he said, half complaining and half groaning, because damn, they *did* make his ass look good.

Raf seemed to pick up on his mixed feelings because he

shot him a cheeky smile, and he half turned, sticking out his ass with a hand on his hip. "Don't you like them, Daddy?"

Brendan still got a rush every time the boy dropped that word so casually. "You know I do, you little tease. But be a good boy for Daddy and take them off, will you? You can't be comfortable in those."

Raf sighed. "They are really tight when I sit," he admitted, already popping the button. He dragged down the jeans, revealing another one of his skin-tight boxer briefs, which showed every line of his body.

Brendan slowly shook his head. "I'm not sure those are much better."

Raf grinned as he dropped his jeans on the floor, then popped a finger behind his waistband and slowly pulled it outward. "These are super stretchy, Daddy. Look!"

Brendan laughed. He was a little minx, his boy. "Daddy will buy you some cute pajamas to wear when you're here because this won't do. But for now, come sit with me."

Raf nestled on his lap, his cute little butt wriggling till Brendan's cock was hard as a rock. "You smell so nice," Raf said with a little sigh. "And you feel so good too."

Brendan held him close, nuzzling his hair. "Mmm, I love having you on my lap, my sweet boy."

"I know I'm really hyper," Raf said, his voice apologetic and with a hint of fear, as if he was scared Brendan would reject him.

"It's okay, baby boy. But how about I help you slow down a little?"

Raf nodded instantly. "My head feels super busy right now," he whispered. "I get really tired of myself when that happens."

"I'm sorry," Brendan said, holding him a little tighter. "But I have something that may help. Two things, actually. I did a little research into ADHD, and I have some ideas that could maybe work."

Raf's head turned to face him. "You did?"

Brendan pressed a kiss on his forehead. "Of course I did. What kind of Daddy would I be if I didn't try to understand you?"

Raf leaned back against his chest, his eyes filled with disbelief. What did it say about what he'd encountered in his life that he couldn't believe Brendan had gone through the minor trouble of finding out more about his ADHD? Brendan's heart filled with softness all over again.

He picked up the small package he'd put on a side table before. "I have two gifts for you. This is the first one."

Raf opened it carefully, frowning in puzzlement as he unwrapped the little fabric square. "What is this?" he asked, clearly uncertain.

"They call it a sensory square. It's made of different fabrics, some supersoft velvet and others a little rougher, and it has all these little ribbons in varying textured attached to it. See? It's for you to hold in your hands and play with, to feel all the different textures. I read that it's often hard for you to focus unless your hands have something to touch and fiddle with, so I thought this might be perfect."

Raf looked at the baby blue square again, stroking a few of the ribbons with his index finger. "Thank you," he said softly. "This has to be the most thoughtful gift anyone has ever given me."

"You're welcome. Hold on to it. Play with it. It's yours now, and you can play with it at any time when you feel restless, okay?"

Raf nodded as he settled against Brendan again, clutching the little patch of fabric in both his hands. His fingers stroked the different textures, finding the little ribbons and loops and fingering them.

"I have something else for you as well."

God, he hoped he'd gotten it right with this one. It was a risk he was taking, maybe pushing Raf a little faster than was smart, but he had to try. He grabbed the pacifier he'd put in his pocket before and held it out for Raf to see.

"That's a pacifier," Raf said slowly.

"Yes."

"It's for me? Like, to use?"

"Yes."

Brendan could say more, like how he'd done research and had discovered some people with ADHD had a strong oral fixation and benefitted from sucking on something. In time, he hoped the boy would consider sucking on something else, but for now, a binkie would have to do.

"Why don't you try it for a few minutes. If you don't like it, no harm done, okay? You can be honest with me."

"It's a little weird," Raf said, his nose all crumpled again.

"Weird is in the eye of the beholder. One person's weird is another person's turn-on or kink. There's no shame in liking what you like, baby boy...or what you don't like. We can try everything and decide to keep what we like and ditch what we don't. Okay?"

"I'll try it for you, Daddy," Raf said, sounding sweeter than ever, and Brendan wanted to kiss him more than anything. But he couldn't rush into that part of their relationship, no matter how much he longed for more.

He took the pacifier from the plastic holder and held it out to Raf. "Five minutes. That's what I'm asking, baby boy. Sit on my lap for five minutes, sucking on your binkie. Okay?"

Trusting eyes looked up at him, and Raf nodded as he

opened his mouth. Brendan popped the pacifier in, a rush of pleasure traversing through him as Raf started sucking immediately. How full his heart was as he looked at the precious boy on his lap, quieting down, now both his mouth and his hands had something to focus on. Maybe in the future, Brendan could give them both something else to keep them occupied, but for now, he was intensely happy to simply hold Raf.

5

It should feel silly, Raf thought. Stupid even. After all, he was a grown-up man, sucking on a pacifier. It shouldn't feel good, and yet it did. His brain tried to fight it, insisting this was crazy, that no one should like this, but his body had different ideas. His body liked the peace this brought, his hands and his mouth occupied, quieting everything and slowing him down.

"So while you sit and relax, I'll tell you a little more about myself," Daddy Brendan said, and Raf sunk against him. "You asked what I do for a living, right? I'm a real estate agent, and I also own several rental properties in the area. I used to be a contractor with my own business, but after I got hurt on the job, I wanted to transition into something a little less physical. I still do a lot of the maintenance on my rental properties, as well as in this house. I like working with my hands, always have. But I run a small but wonderful team as a realtor."

Ref let that sink in as he furiously sucked on the pacifier. It was strange how his body was able to calm down, now that he had something to focus on. He mindlessly played with the little texture thing, his fingertips stroking the fabrics or endlessly fingering the little ribbon loops. He snuggled closer against Daddy Brendan, surrendering to the deep sense of safety and calm. His mind was calming down now as well, the crazy firing of random thoughts decreasing until all that was left was a quiet, happy hum.

"That's it, baby boy," Daddy praised him. "I can feel you relaxing against me. You're such a good boy, listening to your Daddy and giving this a try. I love taking care of you."

Raf blew out a long breath through his nose, then resumed suckling on the binkie. He really should stop telling himself this shit was stupid when it clearly worked. He rubbed his cheek against the soft cotton of Daddy's T-shirt, breathing him in deeply through his nose. The man smelled so good. So safe.

Raf closed his eyes, completely relaxed now. He loved Daddy's strong arms, the broad chest he was resting against, the firm thighs he was sitting on. He shifted a little, his ass finding a large and very hard cock. God, Daddy was so big.

His usual way of getting rid of this much energy when he was this hyper was to score himself a hookup. He'd discovered fucking that excess energy out of his system was pretty damn effective. Hmm, maybe Daddy could help him out here as well?

He repositioned himself, deliberately this time, making sure his ass dragged over that hard dick underneath him. Daddy let out a little rumble in his chest. "Stop teasing me, boy," he said, but he didn't sound all that stern.

Raf opened his mouth to say something, then discovered he couldn't speak with a pacifier in his mouth.

"Uh-uh. No talking. Your five minutes aren't up yet."

If he couldn't use words, he'd have to use other means to communicate what he wanted, right? He pushed off against

Daddy's chest, then swung his legs around him so he was straddling him. It brought his ass in even closer contact with that erection he was so desperate to get his hands on. And his mouth. And his ass, for that matter.

Daddy chuckled. "Are you being deliberately naughty? Do you remember what I told you about what would happen to naughty boys?"

Raf stilled. Was Daddy Brendan really upset, or was this part of their role-play? He peeked at his face from underneath his lashes, and Daddy's eyes were sparkling. Role-play it was. That got him curious. What would happen if he took things a little further? What would Daddy do then?

There was only one way to find out, and before he'd even thought it through, he slowly ground his hips down, causing some serious friction between his ass and Daddy's cock. With only thin layers of clothing between them, he could feel him respond immediately. He hadn't thought it possible, but Daddy's dick got even harder against his ass cheeks.

Raf let out a little groan. He really needed to see that thing in person. Preferably up *very* close and personal. He dropped the little texture thingy on the couch, looping both his hands around Daddy's neck. Daddy's eyes were hot and dark when they met his.

With a slow move, Daddy's hand reached out for his mouth, then popped the pacifier out of his mouth. Raf licked his lips, his mouth strangely empty after sucking on that thing for minutes.

"Daddy," he said, his voice moany and breathless.

Daddy's eyes darkened even more, a low rumble echoing through his chest. It was a sound of want, of need. God, Raf was so on board with wherever this was leading. They stared at each other for two, three seconds more, and then

Daddy grabbed his hair, pulled him close, and crushed their mouths together.

Raf didn't even pretend to resist, opening instantly, the need to taste him coursing through his veins. He wanted Daddy Brendan more than anything or anyone in his life. When the man's tongue found his, he whimpered. He gave him everything he demanded, closing his eyes as Daddy thoroughly claimed his mouth. He tasted as bold as his kiss, dominant yet sweet, hot as fuck and yet careful at the same time.

He pressed his body against Daddy's wherever he could, his hips circling, grinding downward all by themselves, his hands holding on to Daddy's big arms for support. The kiss was everything but Raf wanted more, harder, deeper, fuller.

"We need to slow down, baby boy," Daddy said, panting against Raf's swollen lips.

Slow down? Was the man crazy? "I don't want to slow down," Raf said, sounding downright whiny. "If anything, I want to speed things up. I need you, Daddy."

A strong hand pulled his head back, and Daddy's eyes searched his. "Are you saying that because you think it's what I want to hear?"

Raf worried about Daddy's sharp tone until he saw the genuine concern on the man's face. "I mean it," he said, dropping all whine and pretense from his voice. He reached for Daddy Brendan's hand, then placed it on his own dick. Obviously, it came nowhere near Daddy's size, but it sure as hell rivaled him in how hard he was.

Daddy's expression changed, growing softer and more intense. Raf let go of his hand, but it stayed where it was, cupping his junk and squeezing gently. "What do you want, baby boy?"

"You," Raf said. Then, because Daddy had stressed how

important open communication was, he added, "Your big cock in my ass."

A slow, sexy smile spread on Daddy's mouth. "That's quite explicit."

Raf shrugged. "In the name of open communication and all that."

That strong hand squeezed his junk again, and Raf had to remind himself to breathe. God, it felt so good, that big hand on him.

"I can appreciate that. But don't think I didn't notice that you were naughty, my little minx. I haven't forgotten about that, in case you wondered."

"I really didn't," Raf said, which was the truth. He'd been so focused on moving things along that the fact that he'd wanted to try out how naughty he could be and what the consequences would be had completely escaped his mind. "Are you gonna punish me?" He pushed his bottom lip out in a little pout he knew looked cute on him.

Daddy laughed. "That's not gonna work on me, boy. You can pout all you want and be as cute and pretty as can be, but you'll still face the consequences."

Consequences. Raf swallowed. That word shouldn't sound as hot and sexy as it did. Something told him he would *like* these consequences, as contradictory as that might appear.

Before he could fully process that thought, Daddy let go of his junk, then lifted him up under his armpits and, with one fluid move, laid him across his lap. Oh God. Raf had seen enough porn to know what was coming next. Except this was not some strange fantasy but reality.

Daddy smacked his ass lightly. "Say your safe word for me, baby boy."

Safe word? Were things going to get that intense? His brain latched on to the sliver of fear that rushed through him. If he was going to need a safe word, that meant things might get painful. Had he signed up for that? How was that part of the Daddy-little dynamic Daddy Brendan had promised him? It didn't make sense. If Daddy said he'd take care of him, how could Raf possibly need a safe word?

Those same strong hands lifted him up again and turned him around, cradling him now. Raf was a little scared to look at him, afraid he'd see disappointment in Daddy's eyes, but he encountered nothing but understanding and kindness.

"With the kind of dynamic we have, we move in and out of scenes fluidly, if you can even call them that. But things are about to get more intense, so I wanted to remind you that you can stop everything at any given time," Daddy said, his voice warm. "Me spanking you, sex, even soft commands from me like sucking on a binkie or whatever else I'll ask you. You can always say *pineapple*, and everything will stop. I need to know you understand. You always have a way out if you need time or if something makes you feel uncomfortable, or even if you realize you simply don't want to do it after all."

BRENDAN WATCHED RAF INTENSELY, still not sure if he should proceed, considering the boy's mixed signals. Raf was vulnerable, way more than he probably realized himself, and the last thing Brendan wanted was to take advantage of him. He'd seen how sensitive Raf was to disappointing people, and there was no way he was taking him up on any signals unless it was what he wanted instead of what he thought Brendan wanted.

He'd made the mistake of trusting mixed signals once,

when he'd believed Henry was into the Daddy thing when he'd only been pretending. That part had hurt more than him leaving Brendan, knowing he'd abused Brendan's trust. He'd done things Henry hadn't wanted, not *really*, and he never wanted to be in that position ever again.

But Raf's eyes watered, and his lips curved in a sweet smile. "That makes total sense, Daddy."

Would it ever stop, that deep warmth in his heart whenever Raf called him Daddy? Brendan hoped it would last for a long time, that *they* would last for a long time.

"I'm going to ask you again, baby boy. Are you sure this is what you want?"

Raf's sweet smile turned into a cheeky grin. "Are you now asking for my permission to punish me? Or to fuck me?"

Brendan couldn't help but smile at that mischievous expression. "How about both?" he said, his voice low with want.

God help him, he did want him something fierce. He wanted his hands on him, his cock inside him, his tongue in his mouth, his handprints on that round butt, claiming every inch of his body. He'd never wanted as much as he wanted Raf, and it was a feeling that weighed heavy on him.

Raf swallowed visibly. "Yes, please. I'm serious, Brendan," he said, and strangely enough, it helped that he'd used his given name rather than calling him Daddy. "I want this."

Brendan grabbed that perfect ass, squeezing gently through the thin layer of his underwear. "Have you ever been spanked before?"

Raf's teeth went into his bottom lip as he shook his head. "No. But I told you, I don't really like pain. Or I didn't when that Dom tried some stuff with me. I thought I'd mention it so you won't be upset if it doesn't work."

Brendan's heart squeezed painfully at those words. He still wasn't sure who had damaged Raf to the point where he was this scared of disappointing people, often failing at things, but it hurt Brendan to see. He cupped Raf's cheek. "It's all good, baby boy. Daddy's got you. You have nothing to worry about, nothing to do, except obey me and be honest with me. Can you do that for Daddy?"

Raf nodded, but Brendan could still see the doubt and insecurity lingering in his eyes. How Brendan wanted to promise Raf he'd love being spanked, but he couldn't be a hundred percent sure. It wasn't outside the realm of possibilities that Raf had had negative experiences with punishment as a child, which would prevent him from seeing this as a pleasure spanking rather than punishment. Brendan vowed to make sure he would do whatever he could to make it a good experience for him.

On that note, maybe he *should* mix the two: the spanking and the sex. This wasn't a serious punishment. This was part of the role-play, and he had no intention of making Raf feel like he truly deserved punishment.

"How about another kiss for Daddy? Your mouth is so sweet, baby boy. Daddy can't get enough of it."

That brought a smile out, and Raf leaned in for a kiss. Brendan covered those plump lips with his own, sighing a little when his boy's unique flavor hit his tongue. Raf opened up for him so sweetly, giving him full access. Brendan made good use of it, exploring every little bit of his mouth, of those luscious lips, of his slick tongue, which was so addictive. Fire returned to his belly, to his dick, spurred on by Raf's taste, the little sounds he made, the way he plastered his body against Brendan's.

He couldn't wait any longer and slipped his hands behind the waistband of Raf's underwear, reaching for those round globes. Raf moaned into his mouth, and Brendan answered it with a groan of his own when his hands caressed the velvety skin. He was so perfect, so smooth. He stroked and slid, squeezed and pinched, worshipped and reveled. And Raf responded with sounds—gorgeous, erotic sounds as he moved into Brendan's hands as if in a wordless request for more.

"I want to see you," Brendan said, his lips less than an inch away from Raf's. "You're so beautiful, my boy, so perfect. Can you strip for me?"

He could've easily done it himself, but it was one more step to make sure this was what Raf wanted. It had to be his choice, every step of the way.

Raf slid off his lap, then turned his back toward Brendan as he teased down his boxers. He looked over his shoulder, showing the top of his crack as he sent Brendan a sexy smile.

"You're so gorgeous," Brendan said, wishing he was a poet or a songwriter so he could express his admiration more adequately. Surely there had to be words more eloquent than "gorgeous" to describe the sheer beauty in front of him.

That earned him a big smile from Raf, who dragged his underwear down even lower, revealing the top half of his plump ass cheeks. The skin was as milky creamy as Brendan had imagined. They would look even more perfect with the red of his handprints on them, and he suppressed a shudder of excitement.

"Aren't you going to undress, Daddy?" Raf said with a little pout. "I'm really anxious to get a good look at you as well."

Brendan knew he meant it. It wasn't just a polite thing to say, the obligatory quid pro quo. Raf *meant* it, his hungry eyes dragging down Brendan's body all the proof he needed.

Brendan whipped his shirt over his head without much ado. Raf turned around and let his eyes roam over his chest.

"I love your body," Raf said with such an honest admiration Brendan felt the words in his soul. "You are so big and furry and soft and strong at the same time. You make me feel so good."

Brendan chuckled as he reached for his jeans and slowly dragged them down. "We've only just gotten started, boy."

Raf's eyes had dropped to his crotch where his iron-hard cock had escaped the narrow confines of his underwear and was peeping out of his waistband. The boy licked his lips in a gesture that left little to the imagination.

"Did I tell you I'm a total bottom who loves big dicks?" he said breathlessly.

"You did, but that's information you can repeat at will." A deep wave of satisfaction rolled over Brendan at Raf's blatant admiration of his body. "Are you sure I'm not too big for you?" he asked, only half teasing, as he squeezed his cock in a slow motion that had Raf licking his lips all over again.

Raf harrumphed. "Oh, please, don't be ridiculous. There is no such thing as too big, only not enough prep or lube."

Now *there* was a motto Brendan could get behind. "Show me that pretty butt of yours."

Raf turned his back toward him again and dragged his underwear down, achingly slow, until he finally revealed himself. It was sheer perfection, that plump, peachy ass that was screaming to be marked.

"Mmm," Brendan purred low in his chest. "That's such a pretty sight. Will you let Daddy touch you, baby boy? Make you feel real good?"

Raf turned around, offering Brendan a first peek at his

gorgeous dick. He was small but perfect, hard and already wet with fluids. His skin was milky white all over, creamy flesh with freckles here and there, begging for his touch. He was slim, a little too thin even, with smooth planes of soft skin on his chest and abdomen, not a hair to be seen, with pink nipples that stood at attention.

"Look at you," Brendan praised him. "I've never seen anything more beautiful in my life."

Raf beamed at him without the hint of embarrassment Brendan had spotted. "Thank you, Daddy."

How he needed the praise, his sweet, insecure boy. Brendan debated with himself for a second or two whether he should wait with taking his briefs off, then decided they were way past comfortable what with how hard his cock was, and he slid them off, sitting down as soon as they were gone.

Raf's gaze was glued to his cock, and his mouth formed a little O. "You're even bigger than I thought," he whispered in awe.

"You're even more beautiful than I thought. Come here, baby boy. Daddy needs to get his hands on you."

Raf immediately stepped close to him, and Brendan pulled him onto his lap, needing to feel him. He kissed him deeply as he let his hands roam Raf's body, reveling in the soft skin his fingers touched. His leaking cock bumped against Raf's ass as if signaling the way it wanted to go, but Brendan was determined to get the spanking in first.

He kissed Raf until they both ran out of breath. Raf was already rutting against him, leaving smears of precum on Brendan's body. "It's time for your punishment, baby boy."

Raf looked up at him, his lips swollen and wet from their kiss, his eyes full of trust now. "Yes, Daddy."

6

All his fears and doubts were gone. Raf's head was—for once—crystal clear on what it wanted. He slid off Daddy Brendan's lap, then draped himself across the man's broad thighs. It was a bit awkward, finding a position that was somewhat comfortable, but Daddy helped him maneuver until he was firmly planted on his lap, his ass sticking up.

He wasn't scared, not even a little bit. On the contrary, he *wanted* this. He wasn't sure when and how it had happened, but he trusted Daddy Brendan. It wasn't a rational decision. That wasn't how his brain worked. It was an instinct thing, a deep gut feeling that the man was worthy of his trust.

And so he relaxed on his lap. "I'm ready, Daddy."

"You're such a good boy for Daddy," that low, deep voice praised him, and Raf melted against him.

That was what he wanted, for his Daddy to tell him he was good. His mind, hell, his whole body, latched on to that simple sentence, and it echoed around in his head, making him feel euphoric. He would be a good boy and earn that praise, no matter what.

The first swat jolted him, his body going tense for a second. But then Daddy Brendan talked to him, and he focused on his voice. "You have the most perfect ass I have ever seen in my life. It takes my breath away to see your perfect, smooth skin, so milky white and innocent. Makes me want to do really dirty things to you, baby boy."

Dirty things? Yes, please. Daddy's big hand swatted him again, but it didn't hurt at all. It wasn't that hard, and Raf liked the way his skin started heating up. Another few slaps and, much to his surprise, his body *really* liked this sensation.

"Ah, that's sheer perfection, the way your skin reacts," Daddy said, his voice brimming with pleasure, all low and rumbling like a bear. "Mmm, I think I like your bottom even more when it's well spanked and all red and fiery for me."

Daddy squeezed his left ass cheek, and Raf let out a little moan. His body felt good, even when his brain was still a little confused. His cock wasn't having doubts either, as it was still rock hard. So was Daddy Brendan's, rubbing against Raf's belly, smearing juices all over him.

His right cheek got the same treatment, followed by a few swats to each cheek, and Raf couldn't help but move against the hand that hit him, then caressed him, teased him, squeezed him, then slapped him again and again, covering his whole ass and the top of his thighs. Daddy's other hand was firm on his neck, and somehow, that helped center him. It was his anchor, his safety, and when the sensations got too much, he focused on that.

His ass was throbbing, but not in a bad way. More like it wanted more, but Raf wasn't sure what. Then Daddy's hand left him for a few seconds to come back, slicked up, trailing from the top of his crack downward. Raf whimpered, spreading his legs as best he could.

"Look at you, all eager," Daddy said as he moved his fingers down, way too slow for Raf's taste. Not that he was gonna say that. He had little filter, but he wasn't *that* stupid, not when his ass was smarting from his previous punishment already. Something told him this hadn't been a real one, but if he pushed too far, he'd have to face the consequences. No, thank you.

Daddy's middle finger, all slick and warm, tapped Raf's hole. Good thing he had prepped himself a little before coming over. It was one of the few things he was disciplined about. Now if only he could apply that level of focus to other areas of his life...

"Are you gonna let me in, sweet boy?" Daddy asked, interrupting his thoughts.

Raf didn't say anything, unsure if he was allowed to talk, but pushed back in a wordless gesture. Daddy's finger slipped in effortlessly, and Raf let out a happy sigh. It had been too long since he'd been fucked properly, and he couldn't wait to be split open by Daddy's fat cock. Size might not matter, but it sure as fuck would help him feel awesome.

"Mmm, good boy, swallowing that finger. Think you can take two?"

Damn right, he could. He pushed back when Daddy Brendan added a finger and took them in. God, he loved that slow stretch inside, the way his body hugged those digits, getting ready for more. A little tingle meandered down his spine, nestling in his balls, which were feeling heavy and full. His dick twitched as Daddy spread him open with his fingers, slick sounds filling the room.

Two fingers became three, and Raf was happy as a clam, slightly panting as Daddy Brendan worked open his hole . "Such a hungry little bottom, aren't you? Daddy's gonna stretch you wide with his cock, baby boy," Daddy said in a voice thick with want.

Raf could hear it, the restrained desire in him, and it fueled the fire in his body. How would Daddy take him? On his lap so he could ride him? Or on his stomach on the bed so Daddy could fuck him really deep and hard? On his back so he could see his face?

He'd love that. He wanted to see him when he came inside him. God, he wished he could feel him bare, experience the sensation of Daddy's cum dripping out of him. He'd only fucked bare once, and when he'd confessed it to Rhys, he'd gotten a stern lecture and a trip to a clinic to get tested. Lesson learned. He'd always insisted on condoms after. But now he wished he wouldn't have to.

"Maybe we'll do four fingers next time." It sounded like a promise. "And you may even like my whole hand."

Raf stilled. A whole hand? Daddy Brendan wanted to *fist* him? He swallowed, an electric charge dancing over his skin. He shivered, but not in a bad way, more like... interested? Yeah, definitely curious how that would feel.

"Ah, I see that got your attention," Daddy teased him. He removed his fingers from Raf's hole with a plopping sound. "We'll talk about that, baby boy. Just know I'll do anything that will make you feel good. That's my whole goal, to make you happy."

That concept was completely unfamiliar and strange to Raf. Someone whose sole purpose was to make him happy? To ensure he felt good? What a novel idea. His brain wanted to go to dark places and think of his dad, but Raf pushed it down. Not now. Not when he was feeling so good and was about to feel even better. He could be depressed and lament his asshole dad later.

Daddy Brendan pulled him off his lap, then held him as

Raf swayed a little from being back on his feet. "Let's move this to the bedroom, baby boy. Our first time should be special... and comfortable."

The master bedroom was big and gorgeous, with a big king-size four-poster bed and carpet so soft Raf bet he could sleep on it and be happy as could be. That was until he climbed onto the mattress, which felt like clouds. "This is the best bed ever," he said, dropping onto his back and letting out a happy sigh. "How do you even get up in the morning? I'd want to stay here forever."

Daddy chuckled as he lay down next to Raf on his side, studying him with his head resting on his hand. "Thank you. I paid a lot for it, but it's been worth every penny. I hope we'll be spending a lot of time here."

Raf turned on his side as well, facing him. "I hope so too," he said, then decided he didn't like that they weren't touching and rolled on top of Daddy. He got a wonderful smile in return, as well as the reward of having Daddy's hands on his ass, gently squeezing him. Daddy's big cock was trapped between their bodies, though, and that wouldn't do.

"I'm ready," Raf said, in case Daddy needed one more assurance he wanted this.

"I'm ready too, baby boy."

Daddy rolled off Raf and opened a drawer. Raf recognized the sounds of a condom wrapper being opened, then the slick sounds of lube being spread out. It wasn't long until Daddy positioned himself on top of Raf.

Oh, that was even better, to have that big, strong body covering him. Daddy had chest hair, lots of it, and Raf liked the way it tickled his skin. When Daddy positioned himself, Raf pulled up his legs and spread them wide. Good thing he was so flexible and didn't mind being bent in two. Then that fat cocked bumped his hole, and he stopped thinking about anything else but how much he wanted this, wanted him.

He bore down as Daddy pushed, and the tip of his dick found its way in, stretching him with a burn that spread from his ass throughout his body. Oh, so good, so fucking good.

"Mmm," he moaned. "More, Daddy."

He had to close his eyes as Daddy grunted and pushed in deeper, the sensations too overwhelming. There was the burn in his ass, the fire on his skin, the warmth of Daddy's body, the low rumble of pleasure in his chest, the slick sounds he made as he slowly worked that fat cock inside him, his own little whimpers, which were somewhere between pain and pleasure.

"So hot and tight," Daddy Brendan grunted. "The way you squeeze my cock..."

Raf let out more sounds as Daddy moved in deeper, his skin breaking out in a sweat everywhere. Daddy still wasn't in fully, and Raf breathed in little puffs, focused on relaxing and bearing down. This was by far the biggest cock he'd ever taken, and it required work.

Daddy kissed him, giving Raf time to relax and adjust. It was a sweet kiss, a soothing one that took away the sting of being split open, and Raf sighed against Daddy's mouth, his eyes open again.

"You're being such a good boy."

"I want to be good for you," Raf said, meaning it from a place in his soul he couldn't even grasp.

Daddy cupped his chin as he looked at him intently. "I know you do, sweet boy, but don't ever do something you don't want because you'll think it will make me happy."

There was freedom in these words. Freedom and power,

and a level of care he'd never experienced before. "I want this. I want this very much."

Daddy kissed him again, all tongue and slick and hot until Raf was squirming underneath him. "I know you do. I can see and feel your body responding."

Daddy held Raf's eyes as he moved again, sliding in all the way until he bottomed out. Raf blinked, feeling so perfect and full he couldn't even think anymore. Then Daddy started moving with slow, deep strokes, and Raf squeezed his eyes shut again. His heart rate tripled, his whole body tingling as Daddy pulled back, then surged back in.

Raf shifted slightly, and the next stroke hit his prostate full on. "Oh my god," he moaned. "Oh fuck... Like that, Daddy. Please, right there."

Daddy grunted, then slid in at the exact same spot with slightly more force, and Raf saw stars. They were dancing behind his eyelids, the teasing promise of the whole universe that inched closer and closer on him. He just needed a little more friction on his...

God, yes, like *that*. Daddy Brendan had lowered himself, trapping Raf's cock between their bodies, and he moved against him with every thrust, finally getting the friction he needed. He climbed fast now, his breaths speeding up as the tension in his body grew. His balls clamped tight against his body, and his cock twitched as it got ready for the grand finale.

Daddy Brendan was breathing heavily, his thrusts getting faster, more erratic. He held Raf close as he fucked him deep, using every inch of that perfect cock. Raf opened his eyes. Daddy's face was sweaty and red, his eyes dark as they found Raf's. He felt connected with him more intimately than he ever had with anyone. Daddy seemed to stare into the depths of his soul, his eyes burning hot and full of want and need.

"Are you gonna come for Daddy?" Daddy panted in between hard thrusts. God, the man had power, flexing those hips and slamming deep inside him every time he snapped them.

Raf tensed up, his muscles clenching. "So close," he managed between clenched teeth, unable to relax enough to open his mouth. "So fucking close."

He was almost at the peak, his body hurling toward his release now. "Daddy," he said with a half sob, so desperate to get there. Then louder, "Daddy!"

And then he hit it, his body letting go with a force that made him shake and shiver and scream like he'd never had before. Raf's vision went white, then black as he saw the fucking universe. His balls set off, and his cock spurted out his cum while his ass clenched around that fat cock inside him as if it never wanted to let go.

That must've been the trigger for Daddy Brendan, who let out a low, long groan and jerked inside him, filling up the condom. "Ohhhh, fuuuck," he grunted.

Raf smiled, even as he panted in exhaustion. He'd made Daddy Brendan swear.

7

It had been the best sex of his life. Around him in his office, his team worked hard making calls, scheduling appointments, and answering emails, but Brendan struggled with focusing. It had been two days ago, but his mind kept wandering off to memories of the time he'd shared with Raf.

It was a strange realization that at forty-three years old, this had been the single best sex he'd ever had. And it had little to do with the mechanics, though Raf had taken his cock like he was born for it. No, it was about how being with Raf made him *feel*. Raf's mere presence triggered such a maelstrom of emotions and feelings inside Brendan.

The way his velvety-soft skin had felt under his hands.

How perfect his ass had looked all red and glowing from his spanking.

The trust in his eyes as he'd surrendered to him.

How his body had calmed down after being held while sucking on his binkie.

His genuine eagerness to take his cock... and the way he'd fallen apart while being fucked.

Perfection. Raf was perfection, and every time Brendan had that thought, he had trouble breathing, and his heart did a little jitter. It was the human reaction, he supposed, to dream of something for so long that when it was in reach, you got scared it would disappear again. The thought of messing things up with Raf scared the bejesus out of Brendan. And that was a crazy, crazy thing after such a short time.

He needed to slow down. because he was going too fast. That alone could scare Raf off, although he hadn't shown signs so far. In fact, when Brendan had texted to invite him over tonight, Raf had replied within seconds that he'd love to. But he had to take it slow. He couldn't run the risk of ruining it all by overwhelming him. Raf was new to the lifestyle in general, and even though he was taking to being a little like he'd been born for it, Brendan had to give him time to adjust and get used to it.

"Brendan!" his assistant, Jacki, said in a tone that suggested she'd been trying to get his attention a few times before.

"Sorry, what?" he said as he turned toward her, looking sheepish.

"Where's your focus today, man?" Jacki said, shaking her head. "You've been staring into space all morning."

"I have a lot on my mind," he said, but her raised eyebrow said he wasn't fooling her. No wonder. She knew him better than anyone else. She tapped her foot until he rolled his eyes at her and gave in. "I met someone," he confessed, and her face broke open in a big smile.

"That's amazing!" she said, her tone instantly changing. "Can you tell me about him?"

"He's amazing," Brendan said, a little embarrassed to be gushing about a crush like a teenager. Then again, this was

Jacki, his best friend and the person who knew him better than anyone else. They'd worked together for over ten years now, and she was like a sister to him, the very definition of his safe place. "He's fresh out of college, super sweet, and cute as a button."

"Have you told him what you're into?"

A few years ago Brendan had explained to her what his kink was, and she'd accepted it without questions. Then again, she and her husband were swingers, so it wasn't like the whole concept of kink was a foreign one to her.

"He knows. We actually met at my club. He's new to the lifestyle, but he's taking to it beautifully. You should have seen him as a little, Jacki, the way he lost himself in his play when he was building a train track. It was the single most beautiful thing I've ever witnessed."

Jacki's eyes widened a little. "You're in love with him," she said slowly.

Brendan's heart skipped a beat. "Don't be ridiculous. I've only known him for two weeks."

Jacki let out a huff. "As if that matters. Sometimes, the heart knows. You know Jack and I got married six weeks after meeting."

Brendan *did* know. He'd been there at their wedding, marveling in fate having a sense of humor to bring two people named Jack and Jacki together. "You were older when you and Jack met," he said. "Raf is just out of college."

"I'm not saying he's in love with you. I'm saying I can hear how you feel about him in the way you talk about him, and that has nothing to do with his age. Well, in a way it has because you're attracted to younger men, but it doesn't make it invalid. It's okay to fall fast," Jacki said, her tone serious now.

Brendan leaned back in his chair, rubbing his temples. "If I go too fast, I'll scare him off."

"Good god, Brendan, it's not like I'm telling you you should declare your love for him and propose," Jacki said with a little eye roll. The woman was nothing if not brutally honest and direct. That had to be her Dutch heritage she was always proud of pointing out. "Of course you need to take things slow. But it's okay to feel this way and acknowledge to yourself that you do."

Brendan closed his eyes for a second or two, drawing in a deep breath. "I'm scared," he said quietly when he opened them again. "My feelings for him are big, so big, and it scares the shit out of me. He's everything I've dreamed of, everything I wanted, and now that it's within reach, I'm so scared fate will yank it all away."

Jacki got up from her desk and walked around to Brendan, lowering herself onto his desk so they were close. Her hand was warm and calming on his arm when she spoke. "He's not Henry, Brendan."

A wave of emotion rolled through him. As usual, she'd found the core of his fears. "Rationally, I know that," he said, his voice tight. "But he hurt me so badly, and the scars are still there."

Jacki had been there to help him through the dark days after Henry had left him. After two years together, he'd announced he'd found a better sugar Daddy and had moved in with a rich, older guy who wasn't even a *real* Daddy. Not only that, but he'd told Brendan he'd only tolerated the *stupid little stuff,* as he'd called it, to appease Brendan.

He'd wanted a free ride, a sugar Daddy, and he'd found the jackpot in Brendan, who'd given him everything, thinking what they had was the real thing. He'd been hurt, offended, and left feeling incredibly stupid he hadn't seen it.

In hindsight, there had been signals, but he'd wanted it too badly to recognize them. He'd vowed never to make that mistake again.

She squeezed his arm affectionately. "I know, and that's understandable. But if you want this to work, you'll have to find a way to let go of that pain and learn to trust again. Trust yourself, but him as well."

Her words hit him deep, and he let out a shaky sigh. "It's so much easier for me to show he can trust me than to allow myself to trust him."

Jacki cocked her head as she studied him. "Has he shown any of the signs you saw with Henry, even in hindsight?"

Brendan shook his head. "No. They're nothing alike. Henry was a flirt, and he loved playing games. Raf is... I'm not even sure he's capable of pretense, to be honest. His filter malfunctions a bit at times, but I love it."

She gave his arm a final squeeze before she let go. "You have your answer right there. He's not Henry. Trust yourself with him, Brendan. Don't fuck things up by wanting to protect your heart when there's no need to."

STRANGELY ENOUGH, Raf wasn't nervous when he showed up for dinner at Daddy Brendan's. Maybe it was because he'd focused all his nerves on his job interview the next day, but whatever he was, he'd take it. Daddy had reminded him to take his meds, and he'd slept well the last two days, so he was feeling *good* for a change.

Hell, he'd been pretty much on a high since that amazing round of sex, even if he'd felt it the next day. God, both his ass cheeks and his insides had reminded him of what Daddy Brendan had done to him, but Raf hadn't minded at all. He'd been calmer the next day, more able to focus. Every time his mind had wanted to wander off, the slight sting had helped him refocus and center. Who would've thought?

And Daddy Brendan had clearly enjoyed it as well. Not only had he not said anything when Raf had cursed during sex—something he hadn't realized till later—but he'd dropped the F-bomb himself when he came. Call him crazy —or fucked up, but Raf was really trying to not even *think* bad words out of fear they'd come flying out of his mouth and he'd upset Daddy—but Raf liked having that influence on Daddy Brendan.

When Daddy Brendan opened the door, Raf flung himself at him, needing to feel his strong arms around him. Daddy caught him effortlessly, carrying his weight with one hand while he closed the door with the other. Then both hands held him close as Raf wrapped his arms and legs around that big bear of a body and put his head on Daddy's shoulder.

"Hey, baby boy," Daddy said, nuzzling his hair, and Raf let out a happy sigh.

"Hi, Daddy," he whispered. "I missed you."

It wasn't till his own words registered with him that he stilled. Was he saying too much, too soon? He had to be careful, maybe. He didn't wanna come across as too clingy.

But Daddy simply held him tight, his voice warm as he said, "I missed you too."

Raf relaxed again. Daddy hugged him for a few seconds more before he let him slide down and kissed him. Raf grabbed his face with both hands, loving the texture of his beard under his fingers. They were such a contrast, he so slim and smooth everywhere and Daddy so furry and fierce, and yet they fit so perfectly.

"I made dinner for you, baby boy, so let's eat."

Raf followed him to the kitchen, where something was creating delicious smells that wafted through the kitchen, seducing his nose. Ah, Daddy was cooking something in the crockpot.

"Go wash your hands."

Raf obeyed without even thinking about it and walked to the double kitchen sink. It was easy when he was being told what to do. It brought peace of mind because he knew the expectations and didn't have to guess or remember himself. He so often forgot things, even standard instructions he'd been told a thousand times, and it gave him stress to try and remember them all. This was easy: do what Daddy told him.

"Go sit at the table."

Raf almost skipped over to the dining room, where Daddy had set the table for two. When he saw the two different setups, he stopped in his tracks. Daddy had a china plate with normal silverware, as well as a fancy glass with what looked to be sparkling water with a slice of lemon. But for Raf, he'd set a kid's plate, one of those colorful plastic ones with superheroes on it. Raf slowly walked toward the table, his eyes trained on the plate. He also had kid's silverware as well as a sippy cup. He swallowed.

"I can give you a normal plate if you prefer," Daddy said softly from behind him.

Raf chewed on his bottom lip as he kept looking at the table setup. "This is what you do, right? This is part of being a Daddy and little?"

"Yes. But that doesn't mean you have to agree to everything. You have a voice here, Raf, a choice. I don't want you to do anything you're not comfortable with."

Raf turned around and found Daddy Brendan looking at him with genuine concern. "If that was a reason not to do something, I wouldn't do anything because there's a ton that makes me uncomfortable. Rhys says it's healthy to push yourself out of your comfort zone and try new things."

Daddy gave him a soft smile. "That's true, but you still get to say no here."

Raf swiveled again, facing the table once more. Did it make him uncomfortable? That didn't feel like the right word, but what was he feeling? Surprise, first of all. He could've known, maybe, but he hadn't expected this. But that swirly feeling in his stomach was also excitement. Mixed in with nerves, yes, but he was definitely excited. He *liked* that he had a special plate, that Daddy made him feel special. And he loved superheroes, so that wasn't it either. Then why was he hesitating?

"I think I'm scared of what others will think," he said when it hit him. "I know this isn't normal, and I'm already different than anyone else..."

He choked up, and a soft hand on his shoulder made him face Daddy Brendan. "You don't understand," Raf said, fighting back tears now. "I've always had trouble fitting in. People find me annoying because I'm so hyper, and I'm not a good friend because I'll forget to show up for parties and shit. Stuff, I mean. Parties and stuff. Rhys is the only friend I have, and I'm worried that if I do this, if I embrace this, I'll become even more of an outcast. I don't want to be different..."

"Oh, my sweet boy." Then Daddy's arms came around Raf, and it felt so good to be held. Daddy Brendan put a calming hand on his neck, and his other gently stroked Raf's back until he felt his breathing quiet and his heart rate settle again.

"I won't lie to you," Daddy said, his voice tender. "Most people will say what I do, what I'd love to do with you, is not normal. And many of them will have an opinion and judge. But you know Rhys understands and supports you, and doesn't his opinion matter the most if he's your best friend?"

He had a point. Raf snuggled against Daddy's comforting body. "Rhys will be happy for me. He does stuff that's a lot kinkier than this."

"He does." The amusement was clear in his voice. "And, baby boy, I know this is not easy, but ask yourself if you really want to live your life worried about what other people will think. Shouldn't it be about what makes *you* happy?"

Raf closed his eyes as pain stabbed his heart with an intensity that made him tear up. That was the core of it, wasn't it? Years and years of worrying what would set his father off had left him fully conditioned to care a *lot* about what others thought. How did he change that?

But right now, he had a much bigger problem. A more immediate one, too. He was being difficult, and as a result, he was messing up the plans Daddy Brendan had. His heart felt heavy in his chest, and the happiness from moments ago evaporated.

8

Brendan felt Raf's body tense up. What was going through his boy's mind? Whatever it was, it wasn't good.

"What's wrong?" he asked, still holding him tight.

"I'm sorry I'm ruining dinner," came the muffled answer.

Brendan frowned. Where was that coming from all of a sudden? "You're not ruining anything. The crockpot is set to keep warm, so the pasta sauce will be there when we're ready, and I can heat up the pasta in the microwave. It's nothing to worry about. Tell me what's wrong, baby boy. Please," he added, the gnawing concern inside him growing.

Had he missed something? Had his appeal to not care about what others think been too direct?

"You're not angry with me?" Raf said, still sounding miserable and hiding against Brendan's chest.

"No, my sweet boy. Why would I be angry with you?"

Raf leaned back, and Brendan met his tear-stricken eyes showing his fear and anguish. Brendan's heart clenched painfully. "Will you please tell me what's happening in your brain, baby boy? Because I can't stand to see you this sad and upset."

Raf seemed to search his eyes. "Can we sit on the couch?" he whispered after a beat or two. "Like, with me on your lap? That makes me feel safe."

"Yes, of course we can." Brendan let go of Raf and gently tugged his hand toward the living room. Raf followed him meekly, little left of his usual spark and energy.

Brendan sat down and immediately pulled Raf on his lap, who snuggled against him, letting out a shuddering sigh when he rubbed his cheek against Brendan's shirt. Brendan had hoped for a cuddle session after dinner, so he'd already put out the little sensory cloth. He'd bought two of them, one for Raf to keep with him at all times, and one that would stay at the house. That came in handy now. He handed it to Raf, who fidgeted with it right away.

Raf didn't say anything yet, but Brendan waited patiently. He couldn't rush Raf, not when it was clear something was bothering the boy. At least he was confident it wasn't anything he had done, considering how Raf sought his presence. The fact that he'd admitted he felt safe on Brendan's lap was a big compliment that made Brendan feel warm inside.

"My dad was very impatient with me," Raf said, his voice soft and tight. "I don't know if that's his character or if I bring it out in him because I'm so annoying, but I never felt like I could do anything right."

A pang of pain hit Brendan's heart. No child should ever feel that way about a parent, especially one who was so sweet as Raf. But he didn't say anything, wanting to listen first and get the whole story. Clearly, Raf had more to say.

"I don't think there was a day, growing up, when he would not get angry with me about something. Sometimes it was small stuff, like forgetting to flush or leaving the light on or not remembering to put the trash cans out. I tried to remember everything I was supposed to do, I swear, but it's hard for me. He couldn't understand I didn't do it on purpose, and he'd yell at me over all the stuff he'd told me a million times that I would still forget."

Brendan held him a little closer, his throat getting tight with the hurt Raf was describing. What father would blame his son for something he couldn't help?

"But there was also big stuff, like forgetting the time and not showing up until an hour after dinner. Or not realizing he was on the phone with a client and making too much noise while playing. I'd left the garage door open a few times overnight after playing outside, and even though nothing got stolen, he was furious with me. He always yelled at me, and it made me so scared and I felt like such a stupid idiot."

Things were starting to make much more sense to Brendan now, including Raf's worry he'd ruined dinner. No doubt he'd been accused of that in the past. "Where was your mom in all this?" he asked, trying hard not to make his voice accusatory.

Raf let out another one of those shuddering, sad sighs that broke Brendan's heart. "She was afraid of him as well, so she never said much. Not until he found out I was gay and wanted to kick me out."

"He *what*?" Brendan swallowed back the wave of fury inside him.

"He must have suspected because everyone did. I'm not exactly straight-passing, you know? But he never said anything. Maybe he thought he could scare me straight. I don't know. I sure as fuck pretended to be straight just to appease him."

Curse words were about last on the list of things he cared about right now, and even more after understanding better how Raf's mind worked. "How did he find out?"

"He caught me making out with a guy from my class, days before graduation. Jamie and I had connected at some party and kissed, and even though we both knew it wasn't going anywhere, we were just having fun. So after seeing a movie together, we kissed behind the movie theater, and what do you know, my dad saw us."

Brendan winced. "That must not have gone over well, I assume."

"It was an atomic explosion. He physically dragged me into the car, and when we got home, he still wouldn't stop screaming at me. And I don't know why, but for the first time, I stood my ground. Like, all the stuff he always got angry with me about, I could see it was unfair, but up to a certain point, he was right, you know? I *did* forget shit all the time, so even though his reaction was unfair and over the top, it held some truth. But this, this just made me pause. I can't help being gay. It's who I am, and for him to get so angry—I was drawing the line. So I yelled back at him, and things got ugly."

"Did he get physical with you?" Brendan asked, fear for Raf rolling through the pit of his stomach.

"No. He never touched me. But he threw my clothes into a suitcase, yelling at me to get out of his fucking house, and that's when I lost it. I knew he'd been banging the next-door neighbor for years, and so I told him that he was twice the sinner I was for committing adultery. Turned out, my mom heard, and somehow, that changed something in her. For the first time ever, she stood up to him. She actually kicked him out. I didn't know it, but the house was hers, inherited from her parents, who had passed away young. So he had no choice, not after she called the cops and made him leave. It was satisfying but infuriating at the same time."

What a horrific mess that must have been, to be outed as gay, having to face your dad, and then to see your parents' marriage crash as well. Brendan's heart filled with compassion for Raf. "Are you and your mom good now?"

Raf hesitated a while before answering. "I don't know. I mean, I appreciated her standing up for me, but I guess for me it was too little, too late. One good act doesn't negate all the times you didn't do the right thing, you know?"

Brendan kissed the top of his head. "Yeah, I understand. I'm so sorry, baby boy. You got a rough deal in the parental department."

God, how lucky he had been with his own parents, who'd been nothing but understanding when he'd come out. His mom had walked in three Pride parades with him, sporting a "Proud Mom of a Wonderful Gay Son" T-shirt. It had been too corny to look at, but he'd appreciated it more than he'd been able to say. They still lived in the same town, and he went over at least once a week. Sadly, he knew all too well that his experience was rare.

"I thought that after my dad left, everything would be okay. I went to college a few weeks later, and that was it. Freedom. But it turns out he messed me up good because I still hear his voice, criticizing me and screaming at me."

Raf's voice was so sad. It made Brendan physically ache for him. "Is that what just happened? Why you were scared you'd ruined dinner?"

"Yeah," Raf whispered. "Because you cooked for me and set the table, and then I had to go and mess up the whole schedule."

Brendan took a deep breath and steadied himself. Raf didn't need to see his anger now, the simmering rage for what his parents had done to him. That wasn't what his boy needed.

"You know what we're gonna do? Same as last time. Five minutes of binkie time for you while Daddy talks," he said, already reaching for the pacifier he'd laid out.

The eager way Raf opened his mouth made it clear he was on board, and Brendan couldn't even put into words how happy that made him. Raf started sucking immediately, the pacifier bobbing in his mouth as he furiously put his tongue and cheeks to work.

"Good boy," Brendan praised him. That, too, was something he understood so much better now: Raf's deep need for praise. He'd never gotten it. "So eager to obey Daddy. That makes me so proud and so happy, my sweet boy."

Raf's body completely relaxed against him, and Brendan kept rubbing his back, wanting to use every tool available to make Raf feel special and precious and...loved.

God, Jacki had been so right. He loved him. There was no denying how big and all-encompassing the feeling in his heart was, in his whole body. Every fiber of his being wanted to be with Raf, take care of him, take away his pain and sadness, and make him happy.

He loved him. He loved him so much.

RAF LET OUT a deep breath through his nose, releasing the tension from his shoulders, then resumed sucking on his binkie. With Daddy Brendan's arms around him, his binkie in his mouth, and his hands reveling in the sensations of his texture cloth—which, really, was more like a mini-blankie—his mind quieted down. It was amazing how his stress and worry melted away here in this safe spot.

Was it because he loved being touched? He did, and it was something Rhys had commented on before as well. And Daddy Brendan loved touching him almost as much as Rhys did, though in a different way. God, Raf loved the sensation of being held, of snuggling on Daddy Brendan's lap. The man was a wall of strength and comfort.

Or maybe it was the binkie and the little fidget blankie, both brilliant moves on Daddy Brendan's part. It did help him to have something in his mouth and hands; there was no doubt about that. He tended to get distracted by either talking or his fingers getting restless, and this way, he could calm himself.

But it was more than that. It was everything together, the way Daddy Brendan took care of him. The more he experienced it, the more Raf liked being a little. It was freeing, not having the responsibilities that weighed so heavily on him. And it was peaceful. Daddy knew best, and all he had to do was let go and obey.

Daddy Brendan was nothing like his dad, and if Raf thought about it rationally and not in a fit of panic, he understood Daddy Brendan would never yell at him for forgetting something or for messing up. Now all he had to do was try to remember when his emotions got the best of him. But for now, he just wanted to stop driving himself crazy. And so he did that, letting go of all the worries in his head and snuggling closer to his Daddy.

"That's it, baby boy," Daddy mumbled softly. "That's my boy. I hate to see you so stressed and worried, but thank you for sharing your story with me. I'm so, so sorry for what you went through. I can't take away that pain, but I can promise you I'll never treat you that way."

Raf nodded. He *knew*, even if he'd had a little trouble remembering it earlier.

"But I understand your emotions can overrule your rational brain, so even when you forget, I won't get upset with you. I'll just keep reminding you."

See? That alone proved there was a world of difference between this patient, kind man and his asshole of a father.

"I know you don't know me well yet, baby boy, but I hope you'll give me a chance to prove to you I want nothing more than to take care of you and make you the happiest little boy there is."

Tears welled up in Raf's eyes. When had anyone ever said that to him? When had anyone ever been focused on him and his happiness? It was a whole new experience to be someone's focus, to be at the center of someone's attention. He'd be an idiot to say *no*, even more so because of how much he liked Daddy Brendan. And not just that—he also liked who he was when he was with him.

Daddy had been right. It didn't matter what others thought. If this here brought him happiness—and boy, did it ever—then fuck everyone else. Nothing else mattered but whatever he and Daddy Brendan agreed on. And everything, everything the man had asked him to try so far had been spot on.

Raf's mind went to the beautiful dressing table upstairs, to the drawers underneath it that he knew held diapers. That whole playroom had scared him as much as it had intrigued him, but now he saw it in a different light. He wouldn't have to try everything because it would make Daddy Brendan happy. He would try it because chances were it would make *him* happy. He loved playing with the trains, he loved his binkie and his little fidget blankie, and he loved everything else Daddy had come up with. What were the odds he'd love the rest as well? Pretty big, he guessed, so sign him up.

"How are you feeling now, baby boy? Is your head a little quieter?" Daddy asked, gently pulling the binkie out of Raf's mouth.

"I wanna try diapers," Raf said, sitting up and meeting Daddy's eyes. "I wanna do it all."

Daddy's mouth pulled up in a smile. "That's unexpected. A pleasant surprise for sure, but I didn't see this coming."

Duh, the man had no idea of his thought process. The last thing he'd spoken out loud had been his anxiety and grief over what had happened with his parents. No wonder Daddy was a little confused.

"I was thinking how much I love my binkie and the little fidget blankie you got for me. And I loved playing with the trains and everything else you've had me try. You were right. I was holding off because I was scared what others would think, and that's stupid. I wanna try everything."

"Ah, that makes more sense," Daddy said, his smile widening. "I'm so glad to hear it's connecting with you. But can I ask you a slightly challenging question?"

Raf nodded, curious where this was going.

"In my research on ADHD, I read impulsive decisions are a part of it as well. This feels pretty impulsive to me, or am I wrong?"

Was he right? Raf frowned as he pondered it.

"Rhys taught me a way to test it," Raf said, thinking out loud now. "He said that if this is the first time I'm thinking something and I've never felt that way before, then it's probably impulsive. And he told me never to do anything impulsive that would cost more than fifty dollars or could cause physical or emotional harm to me."

"That sounds like solid advice to me. I'm so glad Rhys has been such a good friend to you."

It hit Raf like a lightning bolt. "I think he's been a kind of

Daddy to me for years. The way he looks out for me and makes sure I take my meds and not make dumb decisions."

Daddy Brendan nodded with a soft smile on his lips. "I had that same thought as well. He definitely has the caring instincts of a Daddy."

"Maybe that's why it's so easy for me with you. Because I loved it when Rhys did it as well, and you do it on a much deeper level."

His mind liked that thought, spinning it around. What made Daddy Brendan different than Rhys, aside from the age difference and the sex?

"The *little* stuff," he said, joy exploding inside him. "The fact that I'm a little with you, that's what makes it so much better. And the sex was amazing," he added quickly, not wanting Daddy to think that wasn't important. "I love the little stuff with you, and I want more of that. So it's not impulsive. It's realizing that something was right for me all along, but I just didn't know it."

Daddy Brendan looked at him with such love in his eyes it took Raf's breath away. Raf had never been very good at reading body language, but this one, even he could interpret. There was love in those eyes, more than he'd ever seen in anyone else's eyes when they looked at him. It was how Rhys looked at him sometimes, but then multiplied by ten.

And then his phone rang, and everything changed.

9

Brendan hadn't let go of Raf since they'd walked onto the cemetery, the boy's much smaller hand firmly encased in his. It had been a rough week for Raf, who'd been devastated by the news that Rhys's father had been killed in a car accident. From Raf's emotional ramblings, Brendan had gathered that the man had kind of been a surrogate father to Raf over the years, providing a shining example of what a good dad looked like. To lose that so unexpectedly had been a hard blow.

Moreover, seeing Rhys suffer so deeply in his grief had been difficult for Raf, who didn't know how to help him. Brendan had encouraged him to simply be there, to be present, and Raf had done so. They'd sat for hours on Brendan's couch, the two of them, sometimes crying or hugging and sometimes quietly chatting and sharing memories.

Rhys had apologized to Brendan for intruding on his privacy, as he'd described it, but Brendan had made it clear he was more than welcome. He understood Rhys didn't want to be home right now, where everything reminded him of his father. And apparently, his mother wasn't taking the news well, even though she and his dad had been divorced for a number of years now. Rhys didn't want to have to be her shoulder to cry on, having enough to deal with. Brendan had taken off from work as much as he could, sensing Raf needed him, and he'd been right.

In a strange coincidence, it turned out Brendan actually knew Jonas, Rhys's father. He was the carpenter who had custom-built the changing table for his little-room, but they'd met for the first time in a club. They'd never played together, but they'd run into each other over the years, and Brendan also had met Jonas's best friend, Cornell, who'd gotten severely hurt in the same accident. He'd liked them both, and they'd shared the occasional beer and laugh.

"I can't believe Cornell isn't able to attend the funeral," Raf said quietly. They were slowly making their way toward the rows of chairs set up for the people attending. They were early. Raf had wanted to make sure he was there when Rhys arrived, who would be riding in the official funeral car. "Rhys said he's not even able to get out of bed, let alone travel."

"It must be so hard for him. Though from what Rhys said, I'm not sure how aware he is. It sounded like they have him pretty drugged on painkillers."

Raf nodded. "He needs another surgery on his knee. They did one right after the accident, but he has complications or something, and he's going back into surgery later today."

Brendan squeezed his hand. "He's facing a long road to recovery."

They walked quietly for a while, Raf's body uncharacteristically calm. "Thank you for everything this week," he said softly.

Brendan looked sideways. "It was my pleasure. I'm so sorry for it all—you know that."

"I know." Raf snuggled closer to Brendan, who put his arm around him and pulled him against him. "You've been so wonderful this week."

"So have you. You've been such a good friend to Rhys. I'm proud of you, baby boy."

"Thank you. I can't believe I even made it through that job interview and got the job."

Brendan had been surprised as well, because he'd kind of expected Raf to either cancel the interview or postpone it. Instead, he'd gone as planned and had managed to get the job—an amazing accomplishment under the circumstances.

"All the more reason for me to be proud of you."

Raf pulled on Brendan's body and made them stop, then turned a bit so they were facing each other. "Daddy, do you think we could spend some time together after this?"

"I'd love that. What did you have in mind?" Brendan had been careful the whole week not to put any pressure on Raf, knowing he was vulnerable and too easily persuaded. So they'd cuddled and taken some time for binkie-lap time, as Raf called it: him sitting on Brendan's lap with his little blankie and his binkie, which they both loved.

Raf let out a small sigh that hit Brendan deep. It spoke of such need. "I want to be a little and have you be my Daddy," he whispered. "I want to not be an adult."

"Oh, baby boy, I'd love that. Let Daddy take care of you, hmm? I've got you." Brendan's heart was so full of love it felt like it would burst. The fact that Raf had asked for it meant more to Brendan than he could put into words.

"I know you do, Daddy."

Raf leaned against Brendan, who kissed the top of his

head. "Let's get through this, and then I promise you won't have to worry about anything for a few hours."

The funeral was heartbreaking to watch, even for Brendan, who hadn't known Jonas all that well. The grief was heavy on his heart not just for Raf and Rhys but also for the droves of people who had shown up, many of whom he recognized from clubs. Ford, Rhys's mentor-Dom, had shown up as well, which spoke volumes about their relationship and how seriously Ford took his training. Raf only left Brendan's side to stand next to Rhys and be there for his friend, and Brendan's heart hurt for them both.

Jonas had been loved, and his friends paid their respects to him in wonderful stories, even if they were heavily edited to befit the audience. Rhys spoke as well, a short, moving tribute to the father he'd loved so very much. Brendan's respect for the young man grew even more when he watched him handle himself so well. He was mature for his age. An old soul, Jacki would say.

Brendan and Raf waited patiently until everyone had left and a visibly exhausted Rhys came up to them. He gave Raf a hug that lasted maybe a minute, the two friends clinging to each other in silent grief in a way that made Brendan's throat tight. Then Rhys turned to Brendan and hugged him as well.

"Promise me you'll take care of Raf," Rhys said, his voice raw and broken. "I need to know he's looked after because I can't right now."

Brendan put a hand on his shoulder. "I've got him. You have my word. You focus on yourself right now."

"And on Cornell," Raf added, an edge to his voice Brendan didn't quite understand.

"Thank you," Rhys said. He studied Brendan for a few

seconds more, then gave him a soft smile. "He's worth it, but I think you've discovered that already."

Brendan smiled back, pulling Raf close to him. "I have. I promise I'll cherish him."

"Daddy will take care of me," Raf said, his voice full of a confidence that made Brendan's stomach flutter.

Rhys kissed his cheeks. "Then you'd better not keep Daddy waiting," he said, then waved them off.

"I'm exhausted," Raf said as they started the drive back.

"I know, baby boy. We'll make sure you get a nap in this afternoon, okay? Let Daddy take care of you."

Brendan loved how automatic it had become for Raf to come to his house rather than go to his own place. He'd barely spent time there this week, stopping by only to pick up clothes and personal belongings he needed. Every night, he'd slept in Brendan's bed, snuggled against him. It was a feeling unlike anything else, to go to sleep and wake up with his sweet boy in his arms.

Raf yawned. "I may need that nap sooner rather than later."

As soon as they got home, Brendan turned Raf toward him. "It's little-time now, baby boy. Let go of everything else and simply let Daddy take care of you, okay?"

Raf nodded, his eyes heavy and his face showing his exhaustion. "Thank you, Daddy."

"Come on, baby boy, let's get you changed into something more comfortable."

As they went upstairs, Raf was quiet and stayed that way when Brendan helped him out of his clothes and dressed him in a pair of Superman pajama shorts. How he wanted to give his boy the sweet comfort of a diaper, but this was not the right time. Soon. Very soon. He couldn't wait to see that cute diapered butt, and he had a suspicion Raf would like surrendering that control as well.

"Go play for a few minutes while Daddy makes you something to snack on, okay?"

Raf nodded, then made his way over to the play bins and plopped down onto the floor. He pulled out the bin with the toy cars, and seconds later, he was on his stomach on the floor, making vroom-vroom noises as he let the cars ride the roads on the carpet.

Satisfied that Raf was okay for now, Brendan went downstairs to prepare a bottle for Raf. That, too, was a step further than they'd taken things so far, but he hoped Raf would take a liking to it. He made sure the milk was warm, but not hot, then went back upstairs, where he found Raf lost in his play. Some of the worry lines on his face were already softening.

When Brendan lowered himself onto the floor next to him, Raf looked up. "I like playing with the cars, Daddy." His voice sounded lighter too.

"Then we'll make sure you can play with them more after your nap. But now it's time for your snack and a nap, baby boy."

Raf cocked his head. "What snack did you bring me, Daddy?"

His eyes fell on the dressing table, where Brendan had put down the bottle, and his mouth formed a little O of surprise. Raf visibly swallowed, but then his face relaxed again. "Okay," he said, looking back at Brendan with sweet surrender in his eyes. "I trust you, Daddy."

The words were right there on the tip of his tongue, but Brendan swallowed them back. It was too much, too soon. He'd scare him off. But he couldn't help the love that had to shine in his eyes. "Thank you, baby boy. That makes me so happy."

They settled onto the bed, Raf between Brendan's legs, leaning back against his chest. Brendan held out the bottle to him, and Raf took it without a second's hesitation. Soon, soft sucking sounds filled the room, and a warmth radiated from Brendan's heart throughout his entire body. What was more precious than this? His sweet boy in his arms, drinking his bottle, surrendering fully to his care. Right here was everything Brendan had hoped and wished for.

SOMEHOW, Raf's brain had clicked into a different mode. Gone was the worry about any of the little stuff being weird or what others would think. In its place, there was a deep desire for more. Whatever Daddy Brendan wanted, Raf was here for it, eager and ready.

He blew out a soft breath through his nose, then resumed sucking and emptied the last bit of milk. He liked it, the bottle. No, strike that. He *loved* it. With his mouth fully occupied, it was like his brain was quieter, especially since he had restricted movement as well, tucked against Daddy's big chest. God, that felt amazing, that broad chest behind him and those big arms holding him. He wanted to melt against him, his body already sinking into a slumber.

The bottle was empty, and Daddy removed it from his mouth. He pushed Raf up a little, and he didn't understand why, until he burped. That made him giggle as he sagged against Daddy again.

"It's time for your nap, baby boy," Daddy said in that wonderful low voice that rumbled deep in his chest.

"Okay, Daddy," Raf said, then yawned. "Will you stay with me?"

"Always."

It sounded so solemn Raf wanted to cry with the perfection of it. But he was tired, so tired, even more so now that his belly was so nice and warm from the milk.

Daddy rolled them both on their sides, then gathered him in his arms again. "Sleep, my little boy. Daddy's here."

Raf was out like a light. When he woke up, Daddy's arms were still around him, soft snores indicating that Daddy, too, had taken a nap. Raf smiled as he stretched, very carefully as not to disturb Daddy. What a wonderful way to wake up, all snuggly plastered against Daddy. God, Raf loved his body. He'd take the soft, furry strength of Daddy Brendan any day over a hard body with a six-pack. On an objective level, the latter might be sexier, but it didn't ring his bell.

And the man's cock, what a work of art that was. It had been somewhat disappointing he hadn't even gotten a second chance to ride it, though he'd understood under the circumstances. He'd initiated something earlier that week, but Daddy had broken things off, explaining Raf was too vulnerable to make good decisions. Raf wasn't sure he agreed, but he'd respected the decision and how seriously Daddy Brendan took consent. But man, he wanted more. More of everything, really.

Daddy's snoring stopped, and he made a cute little grunting sound before his eyes fluttered open. When he spotted Raf, his mouth curled up in a smile. "Hey, baby boy. Did you have a good nap?"

"I did, Daddy. I feel better already..."

Daddy leaned in for a kiss, and Raf obliged eagerly, opening his mouth as soon as those soft lips touched his. Daddy hummed in approval, then rolled them both so he was on top of Raf as he deepened the kiss. Usually, Daddy's kisses were unhurried and languid, but this time, it had a spark, an urgency. Raf felt the same way, as if he had to make up for lost time.

Daddy chased his tongue with his, then explored his mouth with deep strokes while his groin slowly ground into Raf, making him hard, so hard. He felt it build up in his body, this need to be claimed. He moaned as Daddy reached underneath him and grabbed his ass, kneading it firmly.

"Daddy." He sighed into his mouth. "I need you."

Daddy broke off the kiss and pushed himself a little farther up, looking Raf into his eyes as if searching for something. Apparently, he was satisfied with what he saw. His eyes darkened with desire. "I need you, too, baby boy. Will you let Daddy fuck you?"

"Please, yes, Daddy. But, Daddy, can we go bare? I know you're negative because you showed me your results, and you know I am too. I want to feel you, Daddy, all of you... I want to feel your cum drip out of me afterward."

Brendan's eyes darkened even more. "The things coming out of your mouth," he said, his voice low and deep. "You look so innocent, and then you say these dirty things."

"I'm a dirty boy inside, Daddy." With Daddy Brendan, he was. He wanted to do everything with him, try anything the man suggested. "I want to be *your* dirty boy."

Daddy Brendan curled a big, strong hand around his throat with enough pressure that Raf's stomach did funny things. He liked how fragile he felt, how utterly submissive to Daddy. "If we go bare, boy, that means we're exclusive. You and me, no one else."

"I don't want anyone else but you, Daddy," Raf said, meaning every word. "I want only you."

"God, Raf, the things you say. Do you have any idea what you do to me? How you make me feel?"

Raf blinked at the intensity in Daddy's voice, that hand still wrapped around his throat. It was comforting, strangely enough. Arousing as hell too. "Does your stomach do funny things right now as well? Like there's a million butterflies in there?"

The hand on his throat disappeared, and instead, it circled around his neck, pulling him close for a kiss that left him panting. "Raf," Daddy breathed. "My sweet, perfect boy."

He rolled off him, and Raf was disappointed for a second until those big hands dragged his pajama shorts down, taking his underwear off at the same time. He sat up and raised his hands so Daddy could take off his shirt as well. It only took seconds for Daddy to remove his own clothes, and then Daddy grabbed both his legs and bent them backward, taking Raf's hands and positioning them behind his knees.

"Stay like this," Daddy told him, and Raf obeyed. He lay spread out for Daddy, and the weird thing was it didn't bother him at all.

Daddy got up from the bed, and Raf turned his head to watch him. His big cock was hard, jutting out in front of him as he walked over to the dressing table and got something from the drawer. He was magnificent. Again there was that flutter in his belly. How had he managed to find this perfect man?

When he came back, Daddy kneeled between his legs, which Raf kept obediently spread. "You're such a good boy for Daddy," Daddy said, and the praise sunk deep into Raf, igniting places inside him ignored for such a long time. "You're so beautiful, my boy. Every part of you."

He opened some kind of packaging, and then a cold, wet

wipe touched Raf's ass cheeks. Daddy cleaned him up, carefully wiping him down. It was deeply intimate, and yet Raf felt completely comfortable, even with his ass and hole on full display.

"Look at that pretty pink hole..."

Daddy cleaned it with a new wipe, and Raf sighed at the sweet care Daddy took with him. He even pushed in his finger slightly to clean out the outer rim, then dropped the wipes and the package to the floor. Then Raf understood why he'd taken all that effort with the wipes. Daddy dropped between his legs, bringing his mouth to Raf's ass.

"I need to taste you, baby boy. Hold on to your legs."

That was all the warning Raf got before Daddy's hot mouth found his ass. He nuzzled Raf's ass cheeks first, his beard tickling a little. Then his tongue licked up a long, slow stripe downward from that supersensitive spot behind his balls all the way to his hole. Raf shivered at the electric sensation. "Daddy," he breathed, swallowing hard.

"I'm only getting started, baby boy."

Daddy took one of Raf's balls into his mouth entirely, and Raf yelped in surprise. Oh god, that was... amazing, unbelievable. Daddy's tongue teased the underside of his nut, even as it was imprisoned in that hot mouth, and Raf had to dig in hard to stay still. Daddy suckled carefully, with just enough pressure to make his balls tighten in delight. He let it plop out with a wet sound, then gave his other ball the same treatment.

No one had ever done that to Raf, and he lacked words to describe the sensations it evoked in his body. It was as if his body was on fire while shivering at the same time. Little sparks of electricity tingled his balls and his skin, then radiated through his whole body.

"You're so perfect," Daddy said, having let go of his nut. "And you taste amazing."

Before Raf could say anything, Daddy took his cock into his mouth and swallowed him whole. "Oh!" Raf brought out, his eyes crossing at the sensation of his dick in that warm, tight mouth. Then Daddy swallowed him deep into his throat, putting even more pressure on him, and he lost it. He bucked his hips, his ass coming off the mattress, needing more. "Daddy!"

Daddy grabbed his ass with both hands and lifted him up as if he was a buffet, digging in all the way. Raf released his legs, lacking the strength to hold on anymore. Instead, he reached for Daddy's head, lacing his fingers through his hair as he pulled him closer, fucking his mouth. And Daddy let him, encouraging him with grunts.

Raf closed his eyes, his need building so fast inside him he could barely keep up. If Daddy kept at this...

"I'm close," he warned him, unsure if he was allowed to come or not. The lines were not clear to him, but a few seconds more, and the decision would be out of his hands. But Daddy didn't stop. Instead, he pulled Raf closer and increased the suction on his dick. Raf let go, allowing his balls to pull up before exploding into an orgasm that left him shaking as he unloaded down Daddy's throat.

"Ugh," he managed, then moaned as another violent tremor hit him, turning his body into jello.

Daddy let him back down onto the mattress slowly, licking his lips as he watched Raf with burning eyes. "That was a delicious appetizer," he said in that low voice that made Raf want to worship him. "Now let's move on to the next course."

10

Brendan had always loved giving oral, but never more than he did right now. Watching and feeling Raf fall apart had been a precious gift he'd always treasure. The way his boy had trusted him, spreading wide for him and allowing Brendan to bring him pleasure, had meant everything. But Brendan wasn't done yet.

Raf's body had gone slack, and Brendan lowered him onto the mattress again but didn't leave his spot between his legs. He wanted to taste him. *Really* taste him. He was an ass man, always had been, and Raf's round butt was sheer perfection. The skin was so smooth under his hands, like stroking velvet. Brendan hummed his appreciation as he caressed those gentle curves, that unblemished skin.

He pushed back Raf's legs, spreading them wide again. The boy's gorgeous dick was soft now, thoroughly licked clean by Brendan. His cum had been delicious, creamy and tangy. Brendan trailed his index finger up Raf's crack, smiling when that evoked a small shiver. It seemed Raf was an ass man too, only on the receiving end. Another way they were perfect for each other.

Brendan sunk low and replaced his finger with his tongue, licking up Raf's crack. That earned him a moan from his boy, who was still limp, his legs now resting on Brendan's shoulders. "Spread wide for Daddy, baby boy. I want to make love to your ass."

Raf's eyes—which had been closed the whole time, the boy's face blissed out—flew open. Brendan grinned. "Did you think we were moving on to the main course right away? Not a chance, boy. I'm not done exploring yet."

To underscore his words, he lowered his mouth again and let his tongue trail that crack until he hit the jackpot. Raf's breath sounded choked, and Brendan circled that pink hole with his wet tongue. It softened under his ministrations, and he kept licking it, reveling in the sounds that fell from Raf's lips. His body was tightening again, the muscles reacting to the sensations Brendan was creating.

He sucked it gently now, which made Raf mewl like a little kitten, his hands finding Brendan's head again and digging in for purchase. Brendan loved it, loved how his boy physically sought his touch, his presence, even when he was pleasuring him. Raf's hole had weakened enough now for him to slip his tongue in, which he did. He was careful at first, then more confident as he fucked him with his tongue. Raf grabbed his hair in a strong grip that was the perfect mix of pleasure and pain.

Ah, that hungry little hole, so eager for his touch, his tongue, his cock. It let him in freely now. Raf canted his hips and moved against Brendan's thrusts, clearly seeking more. With regret, Brendan let go of him, reaching for the bottle of lube he'd grabbed from the drawer and lubing up his fingers.

He pushed in with two at once, knowing Raf could take it, and he sucked them in instantly, his eyes fluttering and his mouth dropping open in a blissful expression. They really should try how much he could take some time. It wouldn't surprise Brendan if Raf would love being fisted, considering how much he loved having something in his hole.

Or maybe experiment with a large plug, Brendan mused as he fucked him steadily with his index and middle finger, making sure not to curl them. He wanted to build up slowly. Raf couldn't come a second time before he was inside him. Yeah, that would be hot, filling him up with a double load of his cum and then plugging him.

His cock twitched at the idea, signaling its approval. Then again, there was nothing about Raf his cock didn't like. Everything about the boy aroused him from the way he smiled to his perfect bubble butt or how he could suck on his binkie.

"Daddy," Raf sighed as Brendan added a third finger, the boy's hole letting him in with ease. Yes, there was that as well, how Raf had embraced him as Daddy. He rarely hesitated as he called Brendan "Daddy", and it always sounded so *right*, as if he'd done it his whole life.

"I need you, Daddy," Raf said, pulling on his hair. "Now, Daddy."

Brendan didn't usually allow a boy to take charge, but he could forgive it when they were this eager for his cock. "Are you sure about going bare?"

God, he wanted to so badly, but it had to be Raf's choice.

"Yes, Daddy. Only you," Raf babbled. "Only you and your perfect cock, your perfect body, your perfect care for me."

Brendan's heart exploded with love, and once again, he had to force back the words that wanted to come out. "It'll be my pleasure, baby boy, my honor. Nothing between us. Just you and me."

He didn't go slow this time, filled with a need to own Raf All of him. He lined up and pushed inside, that eager hole opening for him as soon as he put pressure on it. He didn't stop, not even when Raf let out a groan, followed by a high-pitched keening sound. He needed to be inside him, to feel him, claim him. Raf was his. His boy.

Raf's body tensed up, but then he bore down and worked with him, swallowing his dick as if he'd been born for it. "All of it, Daddy," he said, his voice still high. "I want all of you."

Brendan surged in deep, grateful he'd been liberal with the lube on his dick earlier. He bent Raf in two, forcing his legs wider. "All of me," he repeated, almost grunting with the effort. "You'll take all of me."

He bottomed out, his balls gently tapping against Raf's ass. He lay on top of him and claimed his mouth, allowing him to get adjusted. But Raf's kiss was eager, hot, his mouth as restless as his body, encouraging Brendan to get to it.

"Fuck me hard, Daddy. No holding back. All of it."

Brendan could see in Raf's eyes that he wanted this. He wasn't saying it for Brendan's sake because he thought this was what his Daddy wanted. He was doing it for himself. He wanted to be split open by Brendan's cock. And he would oblige.

He positioned himself so he had a good grip, then slowly pulled back and surged back in.

"Mmm, yes, Daddy. Like that."

Brendan held on to Raf's legs, then slammed in with full force. The air left Raf's lungs with a whooshing sound, but his eyes rolled back slightly, and Brendan smiled. "Just remember," he said before ramming back in with another mighty shove, marveling at what Raf's slender body could take, "you can't come again until Daddy does."

Raf's fingers tightened on Brendan's forearms. "So good, Daddy," he keened as Brendan found a deep and hard rhythm that shook both their bodies.

Brendan's balls made that delicious wet slapping sound as they bounced against Raf's flesh, and Brendan wished this could last much longer than it looked like it would. An electric charge raced up and down his spine before settling in his full balls, signaling he was running out of time.

He snapped his hips, flexing his muscles as he buried himself deep inside Raf again and again, making the bed shake. Raf's fingers were gripping his arms so tightly they were white, and the boy's mouth had fallen open in a beautiful O, his eyes closed and his cheeks ruddy. He'd never looked more beautiful.

Brendan grunted as he slammed in again, loving the sounds they made together, a sexy symphony that rose higher and higher into a crescendo that had his body trembling with effort. And Raf met him there, flying high with him, his body not only surrendering to Brendan's onslaught but embracing it, welcoming it with every thrust, moan, and sigh.

"Daddy..." Raf wailed, his body tensing up. He was fighting his release, even now eager to please his Daddy. He was such a perfect boy, so willing to obey.

Brendan's balls pulled tight against his body in that delicious mix of pain and pleasure, so full and heavy they throbbed. An electric zing started in his fingertips, then moved inward through his body. His muscles tightened in anticipation, and his last thrusts were anything but graceful as he chased that final step, that last push to get him over the edge...

With one final shove, he buried himself to the hilt inside Raf, wanting to be as close to him as possible when it hit. He let out an inhuman roar when the wave rolled over him, his body exploding in an ecstatic release as it pumped his balls dry with spurt after spurt, deep inside that glorious heat.

"Oh god," Raf cried out, his body shaking as he, too, came. "Daddy!"

Even in his moment of release, the word fell off his lips so easily, and tears burned hot in Brendan's eyes as he fought hard to keep himself from collapsing on top of Raf. His muscles quivered as he rolled them around, pulling Raf on top of him and holding him tight. Raf's head plunked down on his chest in exhaustion, his hot, rapid breaths dancing over Brendan's skin and nipple.

"God, that was perfect. So fucking perfect. I love your cock, Daddy."

I love you. The words were there again, but Brendan held them back, even though that became harder and harder. "I love everything about you," he said instead, because he had to say *something*. Raf had to know how he felt, even if he couldn't share the full depth and magnitude yet. Brendan held him close, his body still flush with perspiration, as they both came down from their high.

"Oh, Daddy," Raf sighed, and Brendan decided they really were the most perfect words on the planet.

11

Raf had only managed to sleep for four hours, too hyped up about starting his new job. No matter how often Daddy had told him he'd do amazing, Raf wasn't so sure. His mind had conjured up about a million things that could go wrong, and he hadn't even tried all that hard.

New things were a struggle for him. He did better when he stuck to routines. That way he had less to worry about forgetting, fewer things to mess up. He could rely on habits. Not that he *liked* routines, but he couldn't deny they made life easier for him.

Of course, starting a new job meant zero routines, no habits to fall back on. During the interview, he'd met the teacher he'd be working with primarily, a fifty-something woman named Dolores Oxford. She'd seemed nice and hadn't reacted negatively to Raf at all. Most people immediately pegged him as gay, but she'd been friendly and engaging, so he could only hope she'd stay that way once she got to know him better. God, his brain had better behave today.

There was little room for error here, or he'd be out of a job faster than he could say ADHD.

Daddy had made him breakfast, then double-checked to see if Raf had taken his meds—he had—and had packed a lunch, which he'd forgotten. The school was only three blocks away from Daddy Brendan's house, and Raf had walked over, and he now stood outside, staring at the building. Nerves barreled through him, making his stomach roll.

What the hell had he been thinking he could do this? His father had been right. He was too dumb for this, for anything. It was only a matter of time before he'd fuck this up too.

"Are you debating whether or not to go in?" a female voice spoke, friendly, though somewhat amused.

Raf spun around and found Dolores behind him, her kind brown eyes sparkling. "I'm nervous," he blurted out, immediately regretting it. He should not have admitted that to the woman who held his fate in her hands.

But Dolores only smiled at him. "You'll do fine. I have an amazing group of kids this year, and they can't wait to meet you. I told them all about you last Friday, and they're excited for you to start today."

Raf swallowed, his brain darting off in every direction. "I'm excited to meet them as well. And I'm glad you have more confidence in me than I have in myself."

Oops. That probably wasn't the smartest thing to admit either.

Dolores put a warm hand on his shoulder and squeezed. "As I said, you'll be fine, Raf. Let's get set up."

Under Dolores's calm guidance, he managed to collect himself a bit, paying attention when she explained the setup of the classroom and what she expected from him on the first day. "We're halfway through the year, which is always a difficult time for the class. It's when the fastest kids grasp the concept of reading, and others fall behind, which can be frustrating for them. I want you to focus on the kids who struggle and encourage them."

Raf nodded, writing it down in his little notebook. That was a habit Rhys had impressed upon him during college: write everything down he needed to do or remember. If he didn't do it instantly, he'd forget.

"We'll see how it goes, but I may have you spend some one-on-one time with a few students and read to and with them. We have some kids from underprivileged backgrounds who could use the positive attention."

"I love reading to kids. I did an internship at a pre-K, and storytime was always my favorite thing to do."

Dolores sent him a beaming smile. "Mine too."

The morning passed in a blur of activities. Raf tried hard to learn the kids' names, but with twenty-three students, that was a challenge. Some were easy, like Alyssa, the cutest little African-American girl who had the most amazing big brown eyes and wanted to be his best friend. Or a mischievous boy named Domingo, who couldn't sit still for a second and reminded Raf of himself.

"Mistel Laf?"

Raf turned around, already smiling. He recognized the voice and the little lisp from Fredrick, his favorite student so far. The little blond boy with the way-too-serious expression and blue eyes that showed his old soul couldn't say the R, which made pronouncing "Mister Raf" a challenge for him.

He sunk to his knees and met Fredrick at eye level. "What's up, buddy?"

"Miss Dolores said you could read me a story?"

The R's were dutifully replaced by L's, and Raf

suppressed a smile. "I'd love to. Did you pick out a book already?"

Fredrick held up a book, a pink and sparkly edition of *The Little Mermaid*. Raf smiled at him. "Excellent choice."

He rose to his feet and took Fredrick's hand, leading him to the reading corner where they found a spot on comfy bean bags. Fredrick leaned against him in a display of complete trust, and a rush went through Raf. At least he was bonding well with the students.

Fredrick listened attentively as Raf read the story of Ariel and even managed to spell out a few words Raf made him try. When the story was over, the little boy let out a deep sigh as he stroked the glittery cover with his index finger. "I like pink."

"Me too," Raf said without hesitation.

"My dad says pink is for girls."

Raf stilled. This was dangerous ground he was treading on, and that on his first day. He'd been assured the school was LGBTQ friendly, both toward staff and students, and he'd ascertained they had not only an official policy that supported that claim but also a history that showed it was more than words. That didn't mean all parents felt the same, however, and clearly, Fredrick's father didn't.

Raf's heart squeezed painfully in his chest as his hand caressed Fredrick's hair. "I'm sorry," he said softly. "Some people can't see that colors are for everyone."

Fredrick leaned back even farther against Raf, letting out a little sigh. They sat for a while like that, and Raf wished he had the words to comfort the five-year-old, whose eyes showed the sadness of someone much older.

"You did well," Dolores said at the end of the day. Raf's head was throbbing with a headache from focusing, but he still managed a smile.

"Thank you. I'm really glad to hear that."

"You have a true gift for working with children. Your mind is creative, and I was impressed with some of your examples, like explaining adding and subtracting by building a train track and taking away pieces."

Raf thought of the train track in Daddy Brendan's playroom. Better not mention that. "Thank you. I love this age."

That earned him a huge smile from Dolores. "I do too. I've been a kindergarten teacher for thirty years now, and I wouldn't switch to a different grade if they doubled my salary."

"Hopefully that's me in thirty years."

Raf left the school in much better spirits than he'd arrived, despite his fatigue and headache. Maybe he could do this after all.

Brendan had underestimated how much his new job would take out of Raf. He'd come home dead tired every day, his face pale and his eyes strained from a headache. He was doing well, it appeared, but it was costing him. Brendan had expected an adjustment period, for sure, for Raf's new position, but he hadn't counted on this level of bone-deep exhaustion that left Raf a shadow of his usual radiant self.

By the time Saturday finally arrived, Brendan was determined to give his boy a full day as a little because boy, did he need it. Earlier, he'd hoped to introduce Raf to his parents, but that didn't seem smart when he was this tired. So he'd called his mom and told her about him. She was dying to meet him, but she also understood when Brendan explained Raf had started a new job and needed some downtime. He did promise her to bring him by as soon as he could.

He let Raf sleep in, smiling with a soft feeling in his belly when Raf finally wandered downstairs at eleven, rubbing his eyes and his hair a hot mess. He immediately climbed onto Brendan's lap and melted against him.

"Hi, Daddy," he said, yawning.

Brendan kissed his head. "Hey, my sweet baby boy. Did you catch up on sleep?"

Raf yawned again. "I think so, but I'm still tired."

Brendan's belly did that funny rolling thing again as he looked at Raf, who had slung his arms around Brendan in full surrender. His boy. His sweet baby boy, who needed him so much. "How about a *little* day today?"

He'd planned to wait till Raf had at least woken up entirely, but he looked so adorable and needy that Brendan couldn't make himself wait.

"Yes, please, Daddy." Raf sat up straight, meeting Brendan's eyes. "A whole day?"

Brendan nodded. "Yes. Let Daddy take care of you. This week was rough, baby boy, and you need to relax."

Raf's face broke open in a smile stuffed with gratitude. "Can we start right now? This must've been the adultiest week that ever adulted, and I'm so tired in my head, Daddy."

Brendan gave him a quick kiss on his lips. "Yes, baby boy. Let it all go. Daddy's got you."

Minutes later, Raf sat parked in front of the TV with a bowl of cereal, watching cartoons. Brendan observed him, smiling when Raf's melodious laugh rolled through the room. His shoulders were already dropping lower in relaxation, and the worry frown plastered on his forehead the whole week slowly smoothed out. It was a start.

After breakfast, he let Raf play with his trains for an

hour. He built an elaborate track throughout most of the playroom, and Brendan's eyes teared up when he saw the pure joy on Raf's face.

"It's time for your bath, baby boy," he announced, and Raf immediately looked up from his track.

"Bath?" *Uh-oh.* Raf's happy smile disappeared. "I don't wanna take a bath. I wanna keep playing with the trains."

Brendan considered it briefly, but then decided he'd played long enough. Besides, Raf was not in charge here, and that had to be crystal clear. No matter how much Brendan wanted to spoil him, it would be on his terms and not on Raf's.

"Maybe we'll have time after your nap, but first, you have to take a bath."

"But, Daddy—" Raf protested again, but Brendan raised his index finger.

"Enough, Raphael. No more discussions. Bath time."

Raf's eyes darkened. "I hate baths."

Brendan mentally fortified himself. He'd known it would come to this at some point, Raf testing his boundaries. "Go sit in the corner for a ten-minute time-out," he told Raf, his voice calm. "If you decide to behave like a little brat, Daddy will have to punish you."

Raf's eyes widened now, his bottom lip falling a little before it quivered. Oh no, he was not falling for this, Brendan told himself. He'd dealt with bratty boys before, boys who would try to play him, and he was on to Raf. Instead, he crossed his arms and jerked his head toward the corner.

Raf cringed, and the look of sheer devastation on his face made Brendan doubt himself for a second. But no, he had to show him that kind of behavior was not acceptable. He stood staring, offering his strictest Daddy look until Raf lowered himself onto the floor, facing the corner. Good. A time-out like that would show him being disrespectful to his Daddy had consequences.

Brendan set a timer on his phone for the ten minutes, then went into the bathroom to make some preparations. He hoped the time-out would make Raf contrite so they could pick up where they'd left off. He set out the three bottles of bath bubbles he'd bought and smiled. Maybe he was spoiling Raf a bit too much by letting him choose in these small things, but he wanted to get it right.

A faint sound drifted in, and Brendan cocked his head. What was that? There it was again, and the blood froze in his veins. Was that...? He listened with all his might, nailed to the spot, and when he heard it again, his stomach turned sour. Oh god. He'd messed up.

When he rushed back into the playroom, he found Raf still in the corner, but his head was buried in his hands, his whole body shaking with sobs he was clearly trying to suppress. "Raf!"

Raf's head shot up. "I'm sorry, Daddy! I'm so sorry. I didn't mean to disappoint you... I'm sorry."

Every word hit Brendan like an ice-cold knife in his heart. He'd gotten it wrong, so horribly wrong. Within a second, he was on the floor next to Raf, pulling him into his arms. Raf still went willingly, but the look on his face broke Brendan's heart.

"My sweet baby boy," he said, his voice breaking. "It's all good. You didn't disappoint me."

There was so much he had to say, but the words wouldn't come, his mind frantically trying to find the right thing.

"But you looked so angry..." Raf cried, the sobs increasing in intensity.

"Oh, Raf, sweetheart, it's me who should be sorry," he whispered as he pulled him even closer, wrapping his arms tightly around him. "I'm not angry with you nor disappointed. I just wanted to make clear I don't tolerate disrespect, but I didn't mean to make you cry or feel so bad."

Raf lost it, and his sobs became deep, heavy bursts of a sadness and pain that originated from a place much deeper than Brendan's punishment. Dammit, he must've triggered bad memories from how his father had treated him. From what Raf had shared before, the man had been a piece of work whose harsh treatment of Raf had left deep wounds.

It took a long time for Raf to calm down, and Brendan merely held him close, whispering sweet words into his ear. The heavy sobs turned to lighter ones, then deep sighs, until finally, Raf's breathing evened out, and he lay boneless, like an exhausted little boy in Brendan's arms. Brendan waited, content to hold him for now and let Raf take the initiative in talking. Or not.

"For as long as I can remember, my dad has been disappointed in me," Raf said after a long time, his voice muffled against Brendan's chest. "I think I've always felt it, even as a little boy. I wasn't the tough son he'd hoped for, the athletic, gifted kid he could brag about. Instead, I was struggling in school from first grade, and I sucked at every sport I tried."

Brendan had to swallow, his throat tight with pain for the man in his arms and the hurt little boy he'd been. He didn't say anything, sensing that Raf needed to talk.

"No matter how hard I tried, I could never please him, never make him proud of me. He always, always found fault with me."

A sigh fell from Raf's lips that held a world of pain. "I didn't dare to come out, knowing he'd reject me for good. All through my teenage years, I pretended to be straight. I doubt anyone in school believed it, but I had no choice. God, I envied Rhys, who casually came out to his parents, and that was that. I yearned for that acceptance, but I never found it, except with him and his parents."

Raf let out another sad sigh that forced its way deep inside Brendan's heart, where it took root. "And I told you about my mom. She never stood up to my dad, not once. I still don't know if she stood up for me that one time because she really didn't want to see me get kicked out for being gay or because she'd learned about his cheating. I think it's the latter, but I don't think it even matters anymore. All my life, I've been nothing but a disappointment."

It drove home once again how incredibly lucky Brendan had been with his parents, who had been so supportive and loving and proud. He lifted Raf's chin with his index finger, meeting a pair of red-rimmed eyes that held too much sadness and pain. "No, baby boy. *They're* the disappointment, not you. They failed you, not the other way around. Parents are supposed to love their kids unconditionally, regardless of what you do. They're supposed to love you for who you are, for the simple fact that you're their child, a part of them. Your parents failed you, baby boy. They're the disappointment."

Raf blinked slowly. "You know, when you say that, I know rationally it's true, but inside, I never stopped feeling like a disappointment. It's proven to be really hard to get rid of my father's angry and disapproving voice inside my head, not to say impossible..."

And he'd just made that worse by making Raf think he'd disappointed him, Brendan realized. "I'm sorry for making you feel like you disappointed me."

Raf's eyes filled up again, and Brendan felt his pain in

the depths of his soul. “I’m sorry I was a brat,” Raf whispered.

Brendan hesitated. Technically, Raf had been disobedient and disrespectful, but how could he communicate that without making him feel like he was a disappointment? “I know you are. But you could never disappoint me. I may be upset with you at times when you act out, but it’s your behavior I’d be angry with, not you. Do you feel the difference?”

Raf nodded, but the doubt was still in his eyes. No wonder. The wounds afflicted by his father were deep, and they would take time to heal. Brendan suspected it would always be a vulnerable part of Raf, an area where he’d have to tread lightly.

He frowned. Was the Daddy-boy relationship making it worse? If Raf had so many negative associations with his father, should Brendan even try to be his Daddy? The things weren’t the same, not on the deepest level, but maybe Raf couldn’t sense the difference.

Or on the other hand, maybe Raf only wanted to be a little to experience what a good dad would be like, and he’d grow out of it once he’d been shown healthy parental care. Where would that leave the two of them? Brendan’s heart felt like a stone in his chest, his heartbeats heavy and oppressing.

12

He'd fucked things up with Daddy Brendan. Raf was certain of it, and he could pinpoint exactly where things had gone horribly off track. He'd been a disrespectful brat about bath time, and Daddy had been disappointed in him. He'd assured Raf he wasn't, but Raf had felt him pull back since.

They'd spent the rest of that day together, and it had been good, but after that, things had changed. They'd been close from the get-go, completely in tune, even when they hadn't known each other well. But now there was a distance between them, a thin layer that showed in formality and hesitation that hadn't been there before. They went through the motions, insofar as that was even possible, considering how short they'd known each other. But Raf felt the true intimacy was gone. There had been no sex, for example. Not even a hand job. Nothing.

Clearly, he'd fucked things up with Daddy, and he needed to fix it before Daddy grew tired of him like everyone else had and booted him out the door. But what could he do? How could he fix this?

He tried hard to be on his best behavior: setting alarms on his phone to take his meds, writing down reminders on his hand to text Daddy as requested or to rinse the plates before putting them in the dishwasher, leaving notes to himself everywhere to put his laundry in the hamper and not forget to lock the damn door. It was exhausting, but he wanted to do whatever he could to make Daddy Brendan happy.

But he worried. Oh my, did he worry. His mind would not let go of the thousands of things it felt he got wrong. Or the things he should improve on, not just with Daddy Brendan but in general. He'd completely forgotten to reach out to Rhys, for example—again—so he felt horribly guilty when he finally remembered to call him. Rhys hadn't been upset, but then again, he never was. At least he'd been doing okay, though Rhys had expressed concern about Cornell's slow recovery.

At work, he forgot things as well. Little things so far, but they had been specific tasks Dolores had asked of him, and he'd seen the slight frown on her face when he'd forgotten. Again. He'd written them down in his little notebook and all, but of course he'd forgotten to actually check. He had to do better if he wanted to keep this job.

"Mister Raf?"

Fredrick pulled on his shirt, and Raf crouched down. "What's up, buddy?"

Fredrick had been slow in making progress in reading, and Raf had been asked to spend at least half an hour one-on-one with him to help him. It was his favorite time of the day.

"I need help." Fredrick pointed at his brand-new, expensive-looking sneakers, which matched the expensive brand of the shirt and shorts he was wearing.

He looked like a little athlete, and yet somehow it didn't fit his personality. Both shoelaces were untied, and Raf smiled. "Let me fix that for you." He quickly tied Fredrick's right shoe. "These are cool sneakers."

Fredrick shrugged. "They're okay."

Raf frowned. "You don't like them?"

Fredrick's eyes found the floor, avoiding Raf's inquisitive gaze. "I wanted different ones."

His voice was close to a whisper. Should he ask? Raf's curiosity won. "Which ones did you want?"

It took a long time before Fredrick said anything, and when he did, Raf had to lean in to hear him. "The pink ones."

Raf's heart hurt for the little boy, and he took both his hands, holding them in a soft grip. "I'm sorry," he said, keeping his voice low as well. It was him and Fredrick now, caught in a little bubble in the back of the class.

Fredrick met his eyes. "Mister Raf, do you know why God made me look like a boy?"

Raf's heart skipped a beat. The way Fredrick worded that indicated far more than an affinity for pink. "Would you rather look like a girl?" he asked, well aware he was treading on dangerously thin ice here, considering what he knew about the boy's father and how he'd reacted to the kid's fondness for girly colors.

"Of course. Because I *am* a girl. I just don't understand why I look like a boy and why everyone thinks I'm a boy. Do you think God made a mistake?"

Raf lifted his eyes to the ceiling in a wordless plea for wisdom. What the hell could he offer this sweet kid, who'd had the bad luck of being born in a family that apparently wouldn't understand his struggle? And what was school policy here anyway? Because no matter how LGBTQ friendly they were, affirming to a five-year-old kid they were in all likelihood transgender had to cross all kinds of lines and boundaries.

He had to say something. He couldn't ignore this silent plea for help, for answers. "I don't know. But you're not a mistake, sweetie. You're beautiful and special, no matter if you're a boy, a girl, or neither."

Fredrick's eyes widened. "You can be something else?"

Oh lord, help him. Now he'd done it. Explaining the concept of gender fluidity or being nonbinary to a kindergartner. How the hell had he painted himself into that corner? In for a penny, in for the whole amount. He might as well finish now.

"Yes. You can be a boy and a girl at the same time or at different times. Or you can be neither. You'll figure it out when you get older, sweetie."

The relief he saw in Fredrick's eyes filled his heart with gratitude that he'd gotten it right, at least toward this little person, who was already struggling to find out how he fit into the world. "I love you, Mister Raf," Fredrick said, and then Raf had two little arms wrapped around his neck and a soft cheek pressed against his. God, his heart, his poor heart. It was exploding with love and compassion right now.

"Thank you, sweetie. You're precious to me as well."

When he let go, he caught Dolores looking at them, a worried frown on her face. The warm feeling in his heart disappeared, replaced by an icy glacier. What had he done?

As soon as he saw Raf's face when he came home, Brendan knew something had happened. "What's wrong?" he asked, concerned something had happened to Rhys or even his friend Cornell.

Raf's shoulders dropped low. "I think I did something really stupid at work today. Something that may get me fired."

"Oh, Raf," Brendan sighed, partially relieved that at least it wasn't something personal. "What happened?"

Raf's cringed, and he avoided Brendan's eyes. The icy hand that had been wrapped around Brendan's heart for the two weeks since *the incident*, as he'd come to call it, squeezed, making it painful to breathe. Had Raf realized he didn't really want a Daddy? Was that why he'd been pulling back?

Then Raf straightened his back, and his eyes filled with a fire Brendan had not seen before. "Do you still want me here?"

The question hit Brendan like a sledgehammer. His heart was squeezed even tighter, and he balled his fists in an attempt to keep a grip on himself. Was this happening again? Was he about to get his heart broken all over again?

"Do you still want to be here?" he fired back.

If Raf wanted to end things, if he had come to the conclusion he didn't really want a Daddy after all, then they'd better break things off now, before Brendan's heart was even further involved. Oh hell, who was he kidding? He'd been all in from the start. He mentally braced himself for the blow he feared would come.

Raf's eyes filled with tears. "God, yes," he said, his voice breaking. "But not if I'm a disappointment to you."

Brendan exhaled, finding the strength to keep breathing. Why would Raf say that again? Hadn't he made it clear two weeks ago that he wasn't a disappointment? Why were they back to this? "You're not. I told you, you didn't disappoint me. That's not how it works with me."

"Then why are you pulling back from me?" Raf's accusing eyes met Brendan's head on.

"I'm not! You retreated from me," Brendan said, his head spinning. What the hell was happening now? It seemed like a bad nightmare, Raf accusing him of the very thing he felt Raf had been doing.

"You haven't called me *baby boy*." Raf's lower lip trembled. "Like, when we talked two weeks ago, I felt like it was all good, but you changed after. You took care of me, but it never felt the same...and you didn't call me your baby boy."

Brendan cringed. It couldn't be, could it? He mentally went over their conversations, his concern increasing by the second as he couldn't remember a single time he'd been verbally affectionate with Raf. He'd taken care of him, yes, but not like before.

"I... I didn't realize," he said slowly, shaking his head as he tried to piece together what had happened. Then it hit him. He'd been scared. Scared that Raf only wanted him as a Daddy temporarily, to fix real-life issues with his father. Scared that what they had wasn't as real and precious as he'd thought it was. Scared that his heart would get broken yet again. Scared that what had happened with Henry was happening all over again, and to protect himself, he *had* pulled back.

"Raf..." he whispered. "I'm so sorry. You're right. This was me. I didn't realize."

"Why?" Raf asked, his eyes swimming. "What happened?"

God, he had to make this right. He owed Raf not only one hell of an apology but an explanation as well. "Baby boy," he started, and Raf let out a choked breath. "I'm so, so sorry. This was all me. Will you allow me to explain?"

"Can we please do binkie-lap time, Daddy?"

The question hit Brendan deep in his heart. He'd failed his boy big time, judging by the pure need in that question. "Please. I'd love that."

When he sat on the couch, his boy on his lap sucking on his pacifier with all his might while fingering his little sensory cloth, Brendan's heart calmed down. It clicked inside him. This was where he was supposed to be, what he was supposed to do. And then the words he'd been holding back so many times came out.

"I love you."

Raf looked up with a jerk, his eyes growing big and his mouth slack, almost dropping the binkie. God, his timing sucked. He fought to keep a grimace off his face. His boy didn't need to see him second-guessing the wisdom of revealing that.

"I love you so much, baby boy, and I'm sorry I messed up." Brendan stroked Raf's back, slipping his hand under his shirt and finding that smooth, unblemished skin. "You see, I got badly hurt a few years ago, and it made me question what we had."

Raf was still looking at him, though he'd resumed sucking. The question was clear in his eyes, and Brendan let out a sigh. He had to come clean here.

"I met a boy in a club. Henry. He was cute and flirty and open for anything, and we soon became close. He said he loved having a Daddy and seemed to like being a little, though in hindsight, I missed clear indications he was only pretending. But he was good at acting, good at making me believe he was happy... Until one day, he left me because he'd found a better sugar Daddy, a richer one, who wouldn't make him wear a diaper."

Brendan's voice broke at the last words, the memory of that deep insult stabbing him in his heart all over again. More than anything, that had hurt, the way Henry had made fun of what Brendan loved so deeply. He'd humiliated him and his kink, and maybe he'd never fully recovered.

Raf grabbed his hand, the distress visible on his face, and Brendan pressed a soft kiss on his hand. "He was only in it for the money… and maybe the sex, because I have to admit we were well matched sexually. But the way he left, it hurt me, and it damaged my trust that someone could really want this, want me. When I learned about the issues you had with your dad, it made me scared that you only wanted to use me to work through those…"

He'd bared it all now and could only hope Raf would understand and, more importantly, would forgive him.

Raf put both his hands on Brendan's cheeks, then pushed himself to his knees to get to equal height and brought their foreheads together. His binkie bumped against Brendan's lips, and he smiled. Raf caressed his beard with both hands, rubbing up and down with soft gestures, and Brendan felt his emotions in each move.

"Thank you, baby boy, for your forgiveness. I never meant to push you away or hurt you."

Raf nodded that he understood, and a weight lifted from Brendan's heart. His smile widened, and when Raf's pacifier rubbed against his lips again, he grabbed the ring with his teeth, making Raf hold position. Their eyes were so close he couldn't even focus, but he felt it, the love in Raf's gaze on him.

When he gently pulled at the ring, Raf let go, and he giggled, a sound of joy that rushed through Brendan. He'd missed that the last two weeks: Raf's happiness. His boy hadn't laughed once. He dropped the pacifier and, instead, covered Raf's mouth with his in a sweet, gentle kiss. Raf allowed him in, his passiveness signaling how much he needed Brendan to take charge, and he understood.

"I love you," he said again, needing to say the words.

Raf's response was a small sigh into his mouth as he plastered himself against Brendan. "Daddy, will you please diaper me?"

13

Raf wasn't sure how it was possible, but he experienced Daddy Brendan's pain physically. It stabbed him in his heart, the crestfallen expression on his face when he'd talked about his previous boy. He wanted to make him feel better, but that's not why he'd asked that question. At least, he didn't think so.

It had been on his mind constantly during the last weeks. He'd even sneaked into the playroom one evening when Daddy had been on the phone with a client. That drawer had pulled him in like a magnet, and he'd caressed the diapers with his finger, imagining how they would look and feel on him. But with the distance he'd experienced between them, he hadn't dared ask.

Now everything had changed. Raf wasn't angry with Daddy Brendan. How could he be when he understood all too well how events in the past could damage you, could make you doubt yourself and others? No, after Daddy had explained what happened to him, it had made total sense. Besides, Daddy had been so apologetic, so deeply sorry.

Oh, wait. Daddy had told him he loved him. Again. That

required a different answer than asking to be diapered. Raf wanted to mentally slap his forehead, but instead, he grabbed Daddy's hand.

"Sorry, my brain got distracted. I love you too."

He bit his lip. His his declaration wasn't exactly romantic, but Daddy's face broke open in a huge smile, those soft eyes of his radiating love.

"You do? Please, baby boy, don't feel pressured to say anything just because I did."

Raf needed to say more words. It was easy for him to forget sometimes that other people couldn't follow his thoughts, which was totally understandable. He sometimes had trouble keeping up with himself.

"I know I can be super impulsive, but I've felt at home with you from the moment we met. Maybe I already felt a little in love with you, I don't know. But I do know that I am now. In love with you, I mean. The way you take care of me, the way you make me feel, I've never been more myself with anyone, with the exception of Rhys maybe. You make me sparkle and shine, and I love who I am when I'm with you."

He frowned as he listened to his own words. Did he do a good enough job explaining himself? The last thing he wanted was for Daddy Brendan to feel like he was being used again.

"I love you for who you are," he added, just to be sure. "And I love all the Daddy-little stuff that we do. I'm not doing that or saying that because I think it's what you want to hear. I mean it, and I hope you know."

There, that was better. One look at Daddy's face confirmed he'd managed to get his feelings across. A big tear dripped down from Daddy's right eye. Even Raf had no trouble interpreting that. That was not a tear because Daddy was sad. That was a tear because Daddy was emotional, because he understood what Raf was trying to say.

"Thank you," Daddy said, and his voice was hoarse. "I love being your Daddy, and I love you, baby boy. You have no idea how happy you make me."

Raf beamed at him. "Does that mean I finally get to try a diaper?"

Daddy's smile transformed into a chuckle. "Are you impatient, baby boy?"

Raf nodded, seeing no reason to deny it. "I really want to try it and share that with you."

Daddy pressed a warm kiss on his lips. "In that case, let's go."

They climbed the stairs hand in hand, Raf walking one step in front of his Daddy. His heart beat fast, and his hands were a little clammy. He was so excited about this next step. As soon as they were in the playroom, he walked over to the changing table, climbed the steps and lay down. Then he turned his head sideways and faced Daddy Brendan, who looked down on him with a proud expression.

"You're beautiful," Daddy said simply, and Raf felt the praise resonate deep inside him. "You're such a good boy for me. Thank you for trusting me."

Raf watched as Daddy unbuttoned the jeans he was wearing, then dragged them down his legs. His underwear followed, and then he was naked from the waist down. Raf shivered as a rush of air hit his groin, but his butt was lying on a soft flannel wrap of some kind, with thin, plastic cushioning underneath it.

"I'm going to clean you first," Daddy announced, and Raf appreciated him explaining what he would do.

Daddy's hands were calm and secure as they cleaned Raf's bottom with a wet wipe. He did his ass cheeks first, then his crack and hole. Next up were his dick and balls, and Raf let the gentle care wash over him. He wasn't hard, but it felt good on a much deeper level. This wasn't physical. It was emotional, soul care, almost. How that was possible he didn't understand, but a sense of peace fell over him as he just lay there and let Daddy take care of him.

He was watching Raf closely, Daddy Brendan, his eyes constantly checking in with him. Daddy reached in the drawer and pulled out a diaper, which he unfolded. Raf's heart skipped a beat. This was it. He couldn't wait to feel it and experience how it affected him.

Daddy lifted his butt up, signaling Raf should help him a little, which he did so Daddy could place the diaper under his butt.

"I'm gonna put some baby powder on you now, okay?"

Raf nodded again, not wanting to break the peace in his head by speaking. The baby powder smelled delicious as Daddy tapped it gently onto both his front and his bottom. Daddy's hands were soft as he rubbed it into his skin with a light touch, and that did make Raf hard. Not iron hard as in "fuck me now or I'll do it myself," but a more gentle erection, one that simply communicated how good it felt. How good *he* felt. Again, he experienced it as much in his head and heart as in his body.

Daddy took his time rubbing the powder in, and Raf could understand why. It was special, Daddy taking care of his boy and Raf surrendering to that care. In a way, this was way more intimate than having sex.

Raf's eyes never left Daddy's face as he finally reached for the diaper, wrapped it around him, and closed the little tabs. He pulled a finger around both of the leg openings to make sure the diaper was comfortable, then wiped off his hands on another wet wipe. When he met Raf's eyes again, the question was clear.

Raf concentrated on his butt, which was now touching the soft material of the diaper. It felt strange, of course, but not for long. More like something he wasn't used to, something his body was trying to figure out.

"Do you want to wear underpants, or should Daddy dress you in your monkey onesie?" Daddy asked. It was his indirect way of checking if he was okay.

"The monkey onesie, Daddy. I love that one."

Daddy smiled as he helped him out of his T-shirt, then held out the onesie and put it on Raf. When he was done, Raf pulled himself up, using Daddy's hands and, with little assistance, climbed down the steps again.

He took a hesitant step, feeling the diaper rub against his ass but, more importantly, against his dick. Hmm, an unusual feeling, but not an unpleasant one. He took a few more steps. Yes, he liked how it felt. He looked over his shoulder at Daddy and gave him a big smile.

The relief on Daddy's face was unmistakable. He stepped close to Raf, tenderly cupping his cheeks and pressing a kiss on his forehead. "I know you had a rough day at work, baby boy. So why don't you go play for a little bit while Daddy makes dinner? Then you can tell me all about what happened."

BRENDAN HAD a dopey smile on his face as he prepared the simple dinner of mashed potatoes, meatloaf, and sweet peas. As a bonus, he had some homemade applesauce, a recipe from his mother that she had perfected over the years. To him, it tasted like home, and he hoped Raf would like it as well. Brendan had discovered that his boy had a bit of a sweet tooth and wasn't too fond of vegetables, so Brendan often had to hide them in some kind of sauce. Hopefully, this would help Raf eat the peas as well.

During cooking, he'd checked in with Raf a few times. He was playing with his cars, enjoying the three-level garage Brendan had found at a flea market a few weeks ago. Every now and then, vroom-vroom noises drifted into the kitchen, widening Brendan's smile. The last time he'd checked on Raf, the stress lines on his forehead had already smoothed out.

Brendan wasn't sure what had happened at work, but he didn't like how tired Raf still was when he came home. Surely that should have been less by now? But maybe a new environment like this was harder for Raf than for others. Something he'd have to look into.

When dinner was ready, he put it on the table, then walked to the playroom to get Raf. His boy had no objections this time and happily obeyed Brendan when he told him to wash his hands for dinner. Brendan couldn't help stealing a few glances at that soft bottom, now showing the extra padding of a diaper. God, he loved seeing his sweet boy surrendering fully to his care.

Dinner was relaxed, both of them chatting about random things. Brendan marveled how easily they moved between personas, Raf especially. He could be a little one second, then switch into something he'd experienced at work. And even more interesting was that Brendan never had trouble following him. It was so smooth, so fluid, that it felt effortless. What a difference from the last two weeks, and Brendan wanted to slap himself all over again for letting it drag on that long.

"How's Rhys doing?" he asked, knowing Raf had called

him earlier that morning. He'd texted him a reminder during his lunch break.

Raf let out a sigh. "He's okay, I think, but he really misses his dad. He's heard from his dad's lawyer about the will, and apparently, he left Rhys everything, including the house."

"Well, considering he had no siblings, that makes sense, no?"

Raf shrugged. "I guess, but I think it still came as somewhat of a surprise to Rhys. His dad was good with money, so this will change his life. He's now a homeowner, and I gotta say, that ranch his dad moved into is amazing. It's way out in the boonies, as his dad always said, but you literally wake up to the birds chirping and the deer grazing on your lawn."

"Is he gonna keep it?" Brendan asked. Raf told him earlier that Rhys worked as a physical therapist in Albany. That commute was doable but not ideal. Besides, a house like that might be a big commitment for a single guy his age.

"I think so, but I told him to talk to you if he was considering selling it," Raf said, shooting a proud smile in Brendan's direction.

"That's very sweet of you, baby boy. Thank you. If he needs anything in terms of repairs or maintenance, let him talk to me. I know a lot of guys, and there're quite a few things I could help him with as well."

Raf opened his mouth to say something, but Brendan shot him a look that he needed to chew and swallow his food first, which he did.

"He may need to make some adjustments because he's thinking of asking Cornell to move in with him after he's been released from the hospital. No, not the hospital, the rehabilitation center. That's where they're sending him first, to learn how to walk and stuff. I don't know, but Rhys said he won't be able to live on his own for a while, so he wants to take him in."

Brendan finished his last bite, then put his silverware on his plate and leaned back in his chair. "That's quite the commitment. It helps he's a physical therapist, so he'll know how to help him, but still."

Raf shifted on his chair, a signal Brendan had learned to interpret by now. It meant he was impatient to say something. Brendan waited to see what was coming.

"He *likes* him," Raf blurted out, looking almost guilty. Brendan suspected this was not something he was supposed to share with people. "Rhys has liked him for years, and that hasn't changed. I think he wants Cornell to move in so he may have a shot with him. Except Cornell doesn't know Rhys is a Dom."

Ah, that made sense. Brendan did the quick math in his head and concluded there was at least a twenty-year age gap between Rhys and Cornell. That in itself was not an issue. He and Raf faced the exact same difference, but the fact that the sub was so much older than the Dom was a little unusual. And the fact that he had no idea Rhys was a Dom was potentially explosive.

"Is Rhys okay with you sharing this?"

Raf looked even guiltier. "Nooooo, but he'll understand I had to tell you. You're my Daddy!"

It was hard to argue with that passionate exclamation, but Brendan sent him a stern look. "I get that, Raphael, but make sure to respect his privacy, okay?"

Raf nodded, then stuffed his mouth full with peas, topping it off with a full spoon of applesauce. Brendan suppressed a smile. At least he was eating his veggies.

After dinner, Brendan rinsed off the plates and put them in the dishwasher while Raf enjoyed his dessert, one of those kids' yogurts with crunch and sprinkles. Brendan had banished desserts for himself years ago, knowing that with his metabolism, he couldn't afford to add that much sugar to his diet every day.

When Raf finished his yogurt, Brendan led them into the living room, where they found a spot on the couch. "What happened at work, baby boy?"

The worry frown was instantly back, and Brendan hated his question caused it, but on the other hand, ignoring whatever was going on wouldn't work either. And so he listened as Raf explained about forgetting things at work and about Dolores, the teacher he was working with, noticing. Just when he wanted to assure him they could find a way to help him, Raf announced there was more and told him about Fredrick.

Brendan's heart hurt for both little Fredrick and for Raf, who'd been clearly caught in an impossible situation. "What else was I supposed to do when they asked me that question?" Raf said, his voice emotional. "I didn't want to lie to them, and I'm not telling a kid they're a mistake. I know this could get me into trouble, but I'd don't know what else I could have done."

Brendan pulled him close, settling the boy between his legs so he could lean back against his chest. "You did good, baby boy. Like you said, under the circumstances you had no other choice."

Raf bit his lip. "What if their parents complained to the school? If Fredrick goes home and tells their parents about the conversation with me, they will be furious."

Brendan pulled his arms around Raf a little tighter. "You have such a big heart. It shows in everything, but the way you talk about them is amazing. If this lands you in hot water, at least you can tell yourself you did the right thing."

They sat quietly for a little while, and then Raf let out a big sigh. "You know how when you're a teenager, you can't wait to grow up? Well, I gotta say that being an adult is not all it's cracked up to be."

Brendan couldn't help but smile at that heartfelt statement. "You can be a little for as much and as often as you want with me, baby boy. I love taking care of you and making you feel happy and safe."

Raf pushed against his arms, and Brendan let go of the gentle hold on him. His boy turned on his stomach, lying on top of Brendan. "I have a question, Daddy, but it's a weird question, and I don't want you to get upset with me."

The qualifier certainly got Brendan's attention. "I promise. You can ask me anything."

Raf peered at him from underneath his lashes. "Even if it's possibly inappropriate?"

Possibly inappropriate? Where the hell had his boy's thoughts gone? "Anything," he repeated, hoping he'd be able to keep that promise.

"I really like being a little," Raf said, lowering his eyes as his hands played with the chest hair that peeked out from Brendan's V-neck. "It makes me feel good inside. Calm and peaceful. And I like wearing a diaper."

As if to prove it, he shifted, pushing his diapered butt backward. Brendan couldn't resist the temptation to place one big hand on that soft bottom, squeezing Raf's ass gently through the layers.

"I'm so happy to hear that, baby boy, because I love seeing you in a diaper."

"About that..." Raf said, and Brendan's brow furrowed. Where was Raf going with this?

"When I'm a little, am I *really* little, or is it role-play?"

That didn't clear much up for Brendan, who was trying

hard to figure out what the issue was. He lifted Raf's head up with a single finger under his chin. "Of course you're not really little. It's a mindset, a role we both play, something we do because you and I both like it. But underneath, you're still an adult. But why are you asking? Baby boy, you're dancing around something you're scared to say, but I need you to be more direct because I have no idea what you're trying to ask me."

"Sex," Raf blurted out. "I'm trying to ask about sex."

And despite the fact that he only had one more clue, things clicked for Brendan. "You are trying to ask if it's okay that being a little turns you on." His hand was still on Raf's butt, and he squeezed it a little harder. "Do you like the way that diaper rubs against you? Is it making you hard, baby boy?"

Relief flooded Raf's face as he moved against Brendan's hand. "So fucking hard."

Brendan smacked his ass hard, knowing that the diaper would lessen the impact. "Language, Raphael," he said sternly.

Raf giggled, a happy sound that warmed Brendan's heart. "That's not helping, Daddy."

Brendan grinned, then grew more serious. "The biggest issue others have with age play is that they think it's perverse and wrong, that we're pedophiles."

Raf's eyes turned stormy. "You're nothing of the kind," he said, a sharp edge to his voice. His fierce defense did something to Brendan's insides, spreading warmth out from his belly. "They don't know what the hell they're talking about and should stay the fuck out of it."

Brendan swatted him again on his butt, a little harder this time. "If I need to warn you again about cussing, you're going to get a punishment you're not gonna like. Am I making myself clear?"

Raf's eyes darkened, but not with anger. "You're really hot when you're strict," he said, and how could Brendan respond to that?

"Focus, Raphael," he told him, trying to maintain his stern look. The little twinkle in Raf's eyes told him he hadn't quite succeeded. He'd better get back on topic before they both forgot what they were talking about. "Look, every Daddy and boy are different in how they incorporate sex into their play. Some keep it strictly separate, for instance, if they have narrowly defined times when they play together. Others have the rule that whenever the boy is in the headspace of a little, they don't have any sexual activities. And some people don't care and mix it up."

Raf looked at him with a serious expression now. "So which are we?"

Brendan loved the impact of that word *we*. "We haven't made a choice yet, so let's decide together. Do you have a preference?"

Raf crumpled his nose in an adorable fashion as he visibly thought hard about it. "We don't really do scenes," he said after a while.

"No, we don't. It's much more fluid with us, with you moving in and out of that headspace."

"So that strict separation wouldn't work."

"It would be hard, I think."

"So the question is if we would feel weird to mix it. Sex and play, I mean."

Brendan was proud of him for grasping what the core of the issue was. "Yes. Imagine, for example, that you're wearing a diaper, like you are now, and I would give you a sexual spanking...or a hand job. Would that make you feel uncomfortable or weird?"

Raf opened his mouth, and judging by the cheeky expression on his face, he was about to blurt out some joke, but then he closed it again. "It's not the right time for a joke, is it?" he asked with a quick look at Brendan.

Brendan cupped his cheek. "I'm proud of you for seeing that, baby boy. It's not. This is a serious consideration for us, especially since we're growing more and more intimate."

Raf's eyes shone. "I like that," he whispered. "I like that there's a *we* and an *us* and that we're making these decisions together. I feel very grown up."

"Me too, baby boy. So tell me what you want..."

That one proved too much for Raf to resist. "I'll tell you what I want. What I really, really want."

Brendan couldn't help but laugh. "I set you up for that one, didn't I?"

"Too easy." Raf put his cheek against Brendan's hand, leaning into it like a little kitten. "I don't know about you, Daddy, but nothing we do has made me feel weird. I love sex with you, and I don't wanna have to schedule that or feel like I couldn't engage in anything out of fear of violating some rule."

"Then we agree. But, baby boy, remember that you now belong to me... and I make all the decisions. You can't touch yourself without my permission anymore. Are we clear on that?"

Raf's cheeks blushed with a delightful stain. "You make the weirdest things sound super hot."

Brendan sent him a big smile. "It's a gift. Now, where were we, because I believe someone *liked* wearing a diaper..."

14

Raf fidgeted as he sat on the floor, playing with his train. It was Saturday afternoon, and he was supposed to de-stress. His mind was anything but relaxed, though. He had a problem. A problem that was getting more urgent by the minute.

He'd worn diapers a few times now, and he *liked* it. He liked how it made him feel when Daddy took care of him. He liked it when Daddy laid him out on the changing table and cleaned him, dabbing baby powder on his butt before putting on the diaper. He liked how it was soft against his bottom and rubbed against his dick. So when Daddy had suggested he'd wear one for playtime, he'd happily agreed.

Except he'd forgotten he hadn't peed yet, a fact his bladder reminded him of now rather urgently. He'd tried to ignore it at first, but he'd had two sippy cups of apple juice and a whole bottle of water, and he needed to go. Badly.

The easiest solution was, of course, to pee in the diaper. That's what a diaper was for after all. But even though he knew that and he liked the diaper, it was a step he found hard. It felt dirty. A little humiliating, even. Because if he did, then he'd have to tell Daddy, and Daddy would have to change his diaper, and that was just...

He cocked his head as he tried to decide how he felt about that. *Unsexy* was the first thought that came to mind. It was a little too close to water sports or golden showers, and while he would never engage in kink-shaming, that was not his thing.

But it's not the same. You're not peeing because the act turns you on or turns him on, or because either of you likes that humiliation. But why then would he pee in his diaper? Where was the attraction in that, the draw for him or for Daddy?

He shifted again, leaning back a little so his bladder wasn't so compressed. Daddy hadn't said anything about it, but Raf knew he was waiting for him to take that next step. He wanted Raf to do this, but why? What was in it for him?

Raf had come to understand Daddy got a deep satisfaction out of taking care of him, ranging from cutting his food into small pieces to making sure he took his meds, ate his veggies, and pampering him with bubble baths and playtime. That part Raf understood, but why would Daddy want to change his dirty diaper?

"Are you struggling, baby boy?"

Daddy's voice startled him, and Raf looked up with a guilty face, knowing he couldn't hide this from Daddy. He nodded, his cheeks growing red with embarrassment at being caught.

But Daddy's face was kind as he lowered himself to the floor right across from Raf. "It's okay. You don't have to use your diaper, baby boy. Not now, and maybe not ever. It's entirely up to you."

Encouraged by the sweet understanding on Daddy's face and in his voice and eyes, Raf let out a breath of relief. "I'm not sure I want to," he said softly.

Daddy took his hand and squeezed it. "And that's okay. You can wear the diaper and take it off when you have to use the bathroom or ask me to take it off. I'm fine with both. It's not a must, baby boy. It's something you can do if and when you want to, when you're comfortable with it."

"I really need to go now."

"Do you want me to take your diaper off, or will you do it yourself?"

Raf loved that Daddy gave him the choice, but he also knew that it was something Daddy loved doing for him. "Will you do it, Daddy? And I want it back on after."

"My pleasure, baby boy."

Daddy's hands were mercifully quick, and as soon as he could, Raf made a mad dash for the bathroom, where he emptied his bladder with the biggest sigh of relief ever. Phew, that had been a close call. A few minutes more and his body would've made the choice for him.

When he was done, he washed his hands, then trudged back into the playroom, where Daddy was patiently waiting for him, his eyes sparkling. "I bet that felt good."

"You have no idea," Raf said from the bottom of his heart.

He climbed back onto the changing table and let Daddy put his diaper back on. When he was done, Daddy leaned in and gave a quick kiss on his lips. "Raf, promise me you'll try and remember you always have a choice. "No" is an answer I will always respect, with or without further explanation. Don't let feelings like guilt push you past your boundaries."

Raf nodded, then raised his head for another kiss. Daddy took his time, claiming his mouth and kissing him until Raf lay panting. It was amazing how a simple kiss could make him want with a fierce need that made him forget about everything else. "Daddy, I want to suck you off," he whispered. "I want to taste you in my mouth, on my tongue."

Daddy's eyes grew hot. "God, yes."

He extended a hand, but Raf grabbed his wrist. "Here. While I'm on this table."

"Raf..." Daddy breathed, then kissed him again, much rougher this time. His tongue pushed into Raf's mouth, demanding entrance, and Raf surrendered, letting him in, as he always did. Their tongues found each other, dancing, twirling, swirling, all hot neediness as desire curled in Raf's belly.

When Daddy broke off the kiss, Raf pushed himself backward until his head hung over the edge, supported by the soft pillow. Daddy let out a sound Raf had never heard from him before, something that sounded a lot like a growl, before yanking his zipper open and dragging his cock out. Raf licked his lips in anticipation, and thankfully, Daddy was impatient as well and stepped close. Raf stuck out his tongue, and with a slow move, Daddy dragged his cock over it from the back to the front.

"My pretty boy," he said, his voice rough. "My pretty boy with his pretty mouth. Are you gonna make Daddy feel good, baby boy?"

Raf couldn't nod, but he could show him, so he stuck out his tongue again. Another drag, and then Daddy tapped his cockhead against his tongue, smearing the first precum on his tongue, his lips. Daddy's cock looked even bigger from this perspective, but that didn't deter Raf. He wanted him in his mouth, wanted to swallow as much of him as he could.

He pulled back his tongue, and Daddy fed him his cock, stepping even closer. Raf's lips formed a perfect O as he took him in, suckling on the head, his tongue charting that unfamiliar territory. Daddy's slit was sensitive, Raf discovered when he tongued it, making a low grunt erupt from Daddy's lips. Raf's cock quivered, rock hard and swollen in his diaper, which was a strange and dirty feeling.

Saliva pooled in his mouth, and he lifted his hand, but Daddy held him back. "Don't. I like you looking all dirty and debauched for me, baby boy. I wish you could see yourself, how obscenely wide open your mouth is around my cock."

Raf canted his neck and opened wide, heat swirling inside him when Daddy carefully pushed in. "You look so sweet and innocent, but inside, you're such a dirty boy. My dirty boy," Daddy praised him.

Raf couldn't do anything but take his cock deeper, sucking as best he could. It stretched him wide, and Daddy was right; that had to be quite a sight. Instead of wiping his mouth, his hands went for Daddy's heavy balls, holding them like he knew Daddy liked, rolling them in his hands with enough pressure to make Daddy moan.

"God, look at you," Daddy breathed. "You're perfection, baby boy. Sheer perfection."

Saliva dripped down his face, probably mixed with Daddy's precum, and he didn't care one bit. If Daddy was happy with him, that was all that mattered. And so he sucked and opened his throat to let Daddy fuck his mouth with slow, careful moves. He never went in too far, never pushing too hard, while at the same time making good use of him.

Raf couldn't take all of him, not even close, but it didn't matter. Within minutes, Daddy was speeding up, the tightness of his balls in Raf's hands indicating he was about to come. Raf's cock was throbbing, and his hole clenched, but he didn't feel empty inside. Not with Daddy's cock in his mouth.

"Raf..." Daddy grunted. "God, Raf!"

Daddy let out a long moan as he came, unloading down Raf's throat. Raf swallowed as best he could but couldn't prevent some of it dripping down his cheek. He must have looked a mess by now, but judging by the fiery look Daddy shot at him, he didn't mind at all

Daddy pulled back his cock, a thread of saliva still hanging from it, and bent over and kissed Raf. He was tasting his own cum. Holy crap, that was hot as fuck. Then Daddy cupped Raf's dick straight through his diaper and underwear, and all thoughts vanished from Raf's head. All he could do was *feel* as that hand increased the pressure, creating perfect friction.

His hips bucked all by themselves, leaning into that touch, into that strong hand. His toes curled, his skin heating up everywhere. He grew dizzy, his head spinning, until Daddy said, "Breathe, baby boy."

Yeah, breathing was good. He tried, but these breathy moans kept falling out, his throat still a little raw from Daddy's cock.

"Does that feel good, baby boy?" Daddy asked.

Raf swallowed, then licked his lips. "So good, Daddy. Don't stop."

"You're still wearing your diaper, baby boy. Do you want Daddy to make you come in your diaper? Are you gonna be Daddy's dirty little boy?"

One second, shame flooded him, but then he pushed it down. No, this was okay, this was between him and Daddy, and if they both wanted this, it was okay. And right now, he could think of nothing hotter than to come in his diaper and offer that, too, to Daddy.

His fingers sought something to hold on to, something to steady him when his body was on fire. He found Daddy's left arm, and his fingers dug in hard, needing to feel him.

The world spun before his eyes, and all he could hear were his whimpers and pleas, these desperate sounds that rose over the sound of his blood in his ears.

Daddy never reached inside his diaper, merely palmed him through the layers, putting enough pressure on it from the outside to make Raf so desperate, so hard, so needy. He scraped his fingers down Daddy's arm, clawing at him. He was so close, so fucking close. Daddy's eyes locked on his, burning with want, and Raf's body surrendered to the onslaught.

His balls pulled flush against his body and then let go, releasing big spurts of cum that jetted out his cock, straight into his diaper. It was strange and dirty and so fucking hot. His vision went white with the force of it. He was still trembling with the aftershocks when Daddy picked him up gently and took him in his arms, only to lower them both onto the daybed, wrapping himself around Raf.

"That, my dirty little baby boy, was the hottest thing I've ever seen."

Raf couldn't agree more.

15

Brendan could tell Raf was nervous about meeting Brendan's parents. His boy kept fidgeting with his hands. Maybe they should've brought the little sensory cloth, but he didn't want to embarrass Raf either. He'd told his parents a little about him and had asked them to be patient. He'd read nerves could make him even more hyper. So far, Raf had been mostly quiet during the car ride, which was unusual in itself.

"Do your parents know you're a Daddy?"

He'd already asked that before, but Brendan understood. "They do, so you can call me Daddy as much as you want to. They also know what kind of Daddy I am, and while they're not sure what to think about it, they've been accepting."

Raf turned his head and studied him. "Did they like Henry?"

Was that what this was, jealousy or a sense of competition with Henry? "My dad got along with him, but my mom didn't like him. In hindsight, that should've told me everything I needed to know."

From the corner of his eye, he caught Raf cringing. "So you're saying it's important for her to like me?"

His voice sounded small, so very small, and Brendan wanted to smack himself for being so careless with his words. He reached for Raf's hand. "Baby boy, she will love you. Be yourself, and everything will be fine."

When Brendan rung the bell, Raf's hand was clammy in his, his boy half hiding behind him. Brendan's heart went out to him. Raf was so very nervous. He consoled himself with the thought it would be over quickly. His mother had never met a stranger, and she'd soon make Raf feel at home.

His mom opened the door with a big smile on her face. "Hello, boys." Her eyes focused on Raf. "We're so excited to meet you, Raf."

Raf stepped out from behind his back. "It's a pleasure to meet you, Mrs. Appelbaum."

He extended his hand, but his mother pulled him in for a hug. "None of that Mrs. Appelbaum now, you hear me? You can call me Mama Laura 'cause you're part of the family now."

Raf's mouth dropped open a little before he caught himself. "Thank you, Mrs...Mama Laura."

It rolled off his tongue a little uneasy, but the start was there.

"Well, come on in. Your dad is already fixing up the barbecue, which I tried to dissuade him of, so no complaints."

Brendan groaned. "Those burgers last time were as hard as hockey pucks."

His mother rolled her eyes at him. "I've been eating your father's overcooked burgers for almost fifty years now. You can damn well suck it up for one night."

A giggle exploded from Raf's lips, and Brendan shot him

an amused look. "You think that's funny? Wait till you try to cut it and need a chainsaw."

Raf giggled again. "I'll just ask you to cut it for me, Daddy."

Brendan grinned. Smartass.

His mother gestured at Brendan with her hand. "Go keep your dad company. He wanted to talk to you about some gutter thing he saw on TV. Utter waste of money if you ask me, but he seems hell-bent on getting it, so I told him to ask your opinion. Please tell him that money would be much better spent on a Caribbean cruise with me."

Brendan hugged his mom fiercely. "I love you, Mom. You're the best mom ever."

His mom gave in and cuddled him close. "I love you too, my boy. Always have, always will. Not sure what brought this on, but you know we're here for you."

With a last kiss on her cheek, he let her go, not wanting her to see how misty his eyes were. How could he explain to her how deeply grateful he was for her, for his dad, for who they were? He'd have to share about Raf's miserable excuse for a father, and he didn't want to betray his confidence. Instead, he went outside as ordered and found his dad on the large deck, fighting with the charcoal barbecue he insisted was superior to any gas barbecue.

"Hey, Dad."

"Brendan. Always a pleasure to see you." His father put a strong hand on his shoulder, never one for displays of affection. His mother more than made up for that. "Has Mom already claimed your boyfriend?"

Brendan looked over his shoulder through the kitchen window, where he could see his mom chatting animatedly with Raf. "The baby pics are coming out any second now."

"She's been looking forward to meeting him."

Brendan refocused on his dad. "I wish we could've made it here earlier, but his job is demanding a lot from him. He's so tired every day."

His dad shot him a quick look sideways as he stirred the charcoals with an iron poker, apparently trying to get them hotter that way. "Is it too much for him?"

He'd told his parents about Raf's ADHD, wanting them to be prepared. "I'm not sure. It's certainly taxing for him."

"Or it could be that you inherited your mother's tendency to be a worrywart."

Brendan smiled. "That's my job as his Daddy, to worry about him."

They didn't talk about his kink often, but he made no secret of it either. "He's into that?" his father asked, but his tone was respectful.

"Very much so. We're a perfect match in every sense."

The poker dropped into the barbecue. "You're in love with him," his father said slowly, turning around to face him.

Brendan nodded. "I am. He's the one, Dad."

His father blinked a few times, then cleared his throat. "We were worried about you after Henry."

His father was a man of few words, but Brendan had no trouble following his line of thought. He'd seen the glances between his parents after he'd told them about Henry and the months after. His mom had outright told him to find the courage to open his heart again.

"I know, Dad. I'm good now. Raf is... He's everything. We're perfect for each other."

A slow smile spread across his dad's face. "That makes me very happy to hear. Now, for the love of everything, let's get this barbecue going before your mother kills me for ruining dinner. Also, I wanted to ask you about this product I saw on TV that promises to keep the gutters clean."

IT WAS impossible not to like Brendan's mom. She's been chatting away with Raf from the moment she'd taken him into the kitchen, handing him a knife, a cutting board, and a supply of fresh fruit, and told him to start cutting. He'd been amazed she'd trusted him with that, and he'd tried hard at first to make the pieces all equal size.

"It doesn't matter, honey. Just cut them down in sizes you can eat in one bite, and it's all good. And don't cut yourself because Brendan will kill me if you get hurt."

He had to laugh, also because it didn't seem unlikely.

She asked him tons of questions about himself, and at first, he was hesitant to answer, convinced she'd think him too young for her son, too immature. But every little crumb of information he gave her, she embraced.

"Brendan was always good with his hands. Even as a kid, he loved woodworking. That, he gets from his dad. Daniel can build anything he sets his mind to. He built this table, for example."

She pointed at a solid wood table in the breakfast area of the kitchen.

"It's beautiful. I'm not good with my hands. Well, I like craft projects, like making funny animals from paper towel rolls or crocheting stuff. That, I love."

His insides clenched as soon as he was done. That seemed not only like a childish thing to love as a grown man, but also a very gay one. Would she judge him?

Mama Laura swirled around and gave him a beaming

smile. "I love those too! I'm a volunteer at the hospital every week, and we do projects like that in the kids' ward."

Raf breathed out with relief. "If you ever need ideas, I have a few books with examples. I love doing these at school as well."

"I'd love that. I have a whole room full of materials if you ever need something. Buttons, fabric, decorative bows and ties, all kinds of paper, you name it. Daniel keeps telling me to throw half of it away, but I don't tell him to reduce the tools in his workshop by half, now do I?"

Raf grinned at that. He loved the little ribbing going on between Brendan's parents.

Mama Laura looked outside the window, then let out an audible breath of relief. "Thank god, Brendan is helping Daniel with the barbecue. I swear, as handy as Daniel is, he's got zero grill skills. Zero, I'm telling you. I love the man to pieces, but I wish he'd let me take over because it would make both of us so much happier."

"Will he let Daddy Brendan grill?"

Mama Laura slowly turned around as Raf's words registered with himself as well. Daddy had said it was okay, but was it really?

"*Daddy* Brendan, huh?"

He squared his shoulders. "Yes, ma'am."

Her eyes grew soft. "It's okay, honey. No need to get nervous. We knew Brendan was into relationships like that, and we're fine with it. He's a grown man, and so are you, so whatever the two of you decide, it's none of our business. All I want is for him to be happy."

Raf looked at her, her kind eyes, which reminded him of Daddy, the gentle smile on her lips, which showed how much she loved her son, and the utter and complete acceptance in her voice. It wasn't fair to compare, but how could he not when it was all he could think about?

"He's lucky to have you," he said, his voice breaking a little.

She stepped close to him but didn't touch him. "We're blessed to have him. He's a wonderful man, Raf, and I couldn't be prouder to be his mom."

He swallowed. "Even though he's gay? Even though he's my Daddy?"

Mama Laura gently shook her head, her eyes so much like Daddy Brendan's that Raf felt the love pouring out from them. "Neither of those matter to us. He's my son, and I would've loved him no matter what, but he's become a man I'm proud of. He's kind, gentle, caring, and he takes great care of the people he loves. What more could I ask for?"

Raf wiped away the single tear that popped out of his right eye. "He's in love with me."

Mama Laura's smile widened. "I know, honey. I could hear that from the moment he told me about you, and I can see it clear as day in how he looks at you. He's got stars in his eyes."

Raf smiled. He liked that expression. It reminded him of the cartoons he loved watching. "I love him too."

"I could see that as soon as you walked in. You're all starry-eyed yourself, honey."

"I've never felt this way before. It's a little scary."

She reached for him, but slowly, as if giving him time to step back or refuse her touch. But he stood there and accepted her hand, which caressed his cheek. "Love is supposed to be scary. If it feels too safe and comfortable, especially in the beginning, I'd be worried."

That made sense, didn't it? "I don't trust people easily, but I do trust D... Brendan."

"You can call him Daddy, honey. It doesn't bother me at all," Mama Laura said, and Raf had to fight hard to push back more tears. He was not going to cry in front of Mama Laura. Not even if she made him feel all the things about what a mama was supposed to be like.

"Thank you," he managed. "Thank you for raising such a wonderful son and for making me feel welcome. I was really nervous about meeting you."

She caressed his cheek one more time, then leaned in and pressed a warm kiss on it. "We love you already, honey. You make my boy's eyes sparkle, and that's all I needed to love you. But the fact that you're so sweet makes it even easier. Now, let's finish this fruit salad because I swear, you're gonna need it to wash down the burgers."

16

Life should have been perfect, what with Daddy Brendan taking such good care of him and his new job and all, and yet Raf still felt unsettled. Meeting Daddy's parents had been all kinds of wonderful, though Mama Laura had been right: the burgers were close to inedible. Raf had tried valiantly to eat them, but they had been so hard to chew. When he'd looked away from his plate for a second and then looked back, the remainder of his burger had disappeared. Daddy Brendan had winked at him, and Raf had been so grateful his heart felt like bursting.

Daddy's parents had been so nice to him, so kind and loving, that he couldn't wait to see them again. Mama Laura had swapped phone numbers with him and had already texted him a bunch of times with ideas for crafts and what did he think? He'd sent her some links to websites with great ideas and had been ten kinds of happy with her gratitude and praise for him.

But despite all that, he wasn't truly happy. Something dark loomed in his heart, like a stubborn black cloud that refused to budge. He kept telling himself he should be happy because he had it all, but his soul wasn't convinced. It hurt inside, and no matter how hard he tried, he couldn't ignore it. Couldn't ignore the memories that kept popping up, the voice that played in his head on a near-constant loop.

You'll never amount to anything if you don't get your act together.

If you tried harder, you could remember things.

That whole ADHD thing is bullshit. It's just an excuse for being undisciplined and lazy.

You'll never get into college if you don't work harder.

Would he ever be free of his father's voice?

To make matters worse, just when he thought he'd at least gotten away with his controversial discussion with Fredrick, Dolores took him aside after class and told him the principal wanted to talk to him. It had been three weeks, and he'd really thought Fredrick hadn't mentioned it to their parents. Dammit.

"Do you know what it's about?" he dared to ask Dolores.

Her eyes were sad. "I think you and I both know. I'm sorry, Raf. It was a tough position for you to be in."

Raf pushed out a breath between his lips. "Did you know about them? About Fredrick being transgender?"

"That's a bold conclusion based on how short you've known him."

Raf shook his head. "You knew. You had to know. It's so obvious."

"Maybe, but his parents are conservative, very religious as well. What good does it do to talk about it with him, knowing there is no way he'd be able to express himself at home?"

Raf crossed his arms, refusing to give in to that easy argument. "At least Fredrick knows they're not alone, that someone understands them. Sometimes, that's all you need to survive."

He thought of Rhys, who had stood by him during his difficult teenage years. No matter what his father had slung at him, Rhys had been his anchor, his daily reminder that he was okay the way he was, even if he couldn't be himself at home. If he had provided that for Fredrick, if only for a few minutes, it would've been worth it.

Dolores put a soft hand on Raf's shoulder. "I understand where you're coming from, but I've learned to pick my battles. It won't help the kids if I get fired over an incident like this either, you know?"

He did know, and he did understand the point she was making. But he couldn't help but feel it was a little easy, a little too comfortable. If everyone felt that way, there would never be a change for the better for transgender students or gay students or students who fell outside what was considered the norm in whatever way. Someone had to stand up and make that change, and it looked like it had to be him in this case.

With lead in his shoes, he made his way to the principal's office. He wiped his clammy hands off on his jeans before knocking.

"Come on in," the principal called out. Principal Williams was a kind but somewhat stern man in his late forties, if Raf had to guess. Raf'd had little interaction with him so far after the job interview, but the man was nice enough, and he had hired him, so there was that.

"I was told you wanted to see me," Raf said, suddenly feeling like a teenager again who got called into the principal's office.

"Raf, yes. Thanks for stopping by. Can you close the door behind you?"

Yeah, that wasn't a good sign, that closed door. Raf did as he asked, then settled down on a chair the principal indicated.

"Do you have any idea of why I called you in?"

Raf couldn't help but smile. "That line hasn't worked on me since I was a teen. I'm not incriminating myself."

That earned him a chuckle from Williams. "Sorry, force of habit with students." He lowered himself on a chair across from Raf, then folded his hands as he met his eyes. "I received a rather concerned call from the parents of Fredrick Whipple. They claimed you had an inappropriate conversation with their son. Would you care to shed some light on that?"

Raf hesitated. Technically, the principal still hadn't said what exactly he'd done wrong, except for that label "inappropriate conversation." He could try and play dumb, but chances were that wouldn't get him anywhere. No, he was better off being honest and transparent about it. If the principal felt Raf had nothing to hide, that might make a better impression.

"I wouldn't call it inappropriate. Fredrick asked me some questions about gender, and I answered them as best I could."

Williams let out a subtle sigh. "Part of me had hoped you would simply deny it because that would've been easier. But I appreciate you being honest with me. Can you tell me what the conversation was about?"

Raf summarized his talk with Fredrick to the best of his recollection. Remembering exact words was always hard for him, so he hoped he'd quoted both of them correctly. "I didn't tell them anything they didn't ask me. I simply tried to answer their questions and reassure them."

"I understand, but his parents feel like you crossed a

line. Apparently, Fredrick told them that he's a girl and that you told him that was okay."

Raf straightened his back. "I think they might be, and it is okay. It's who they are."

"*They*?"

Raf shrugged. "It's a simple matter of respect. Since Fredrick seems convinced they're not a boy, I figured I'd refer to them as they."

Williams's face tightened in a frown. "I think that's jumping the gun, wouldn't you say?"

"Using correct pronouns that match the gender someone identifies with is a powerful tool. Research has shown how important this is for the emotional well-being of transgender, gender-fluid, or nonbinary people."

"I think my point is that you're not qualified to determine whether or not Fredrick is any of those. He's five years old. Certainly that's too young to know anything, let alone something society has made as complicated as gender."

And with those words, Raf knew he didn't have an ally in Williams. Not a true one, anyway. The man might be principal of the school that on paper had a solid LGBT-affirming policy, but his own convictions weren't as progressive.

"On that, we'll have to agree to disagree. I knew I was gay at that age, and there was nothing complicated about it. I might not have known the label yet, but I certainly knew I was different than everyone else. Fredrick knows as well. They know they're not a boy, and we have to respect that. In my opinion."

Williams leaned back in his chair. "I understand why this student may strike a personal chord with you, but it's important for us as staff to keep a professional distance. The parents are the primary caretakers and are fully empowered to make important decisions, especially on complicated and moral issues like this."

Raf shook his head. "It's not that complicated, and it's certainly not a moral issue. It's who they are, an identity issue. And it shouldn't even be an issue, not in a school that has a policy that clearly states transgender students are not only welcomed but embraced, no matter where they are in their journey."

William slowly nodded. "True, but our starting point is always to respect the parents' wishes. If the parents are not on board with it, we're not going to set a different course than they are. And that's the case with Fredrick. His parents insist we treat him as a boy in every aspect and refrain from any discussions about gender with him."

Even though it was subtly formulated, Raf recognized the warning behind it. "So what do I do if he asks me questions?"

"That won't be an issue since he'll be transferred to Mrs. Chandler's class. His parents didn't feel like Mrs. Oxford's class was a good fit for him."

"Because of me," Raf said, finding it hard to speak. Sadness curled itself around his throat.

"I hope you learn from this, Raf. You have a gift for working with children. Dolores says the same. I would be sad to see you leave this school because of misunderstandings like this."

Raf knew when he was being dismissed, and the conversation wrapped up shortly after.

His heart was heavy as he walked home. He thought he'd done the right thing, but now he wasn't so sure anymore. How was any of this fair? It wasn't, not to him and especially not to Fredrick, who had bonded so closely with him. He couldn't believe he'd never get to spend time with them again. He'd miss them.

How sad was it that with all the progress society had claimed to make, things like this still happened? Fifteen or so years ago, he'd been in that exact same position with his dad, so why had nothing changed? Why were people still insisting on being so backward and hateful? It didn't make sense to him.

He could only imagine what growing up would be like for Fredrick, based on his own experiences. Would they ever get to be themselves? Or would they, too, have to wait until they were legal adults, until they left for college? Were they even safe at home?

His own father had never hit him, but he had still done enough damage, and it had been on Raf's mind more than ever lately. The deep insecurity he had, for example, the constant fear that Daddy Brendan would grow disappointed with him, would reject him too. Would that ever go away?

It was such a hard thing to grasp, to be so happy and to be so frustrated and sad at the same time. He wanted to be completely happy, to forget about his past, but he couldn't. It kept popping up, and this whole sad situation with Fredrick only brought it back to the surface.

And as much as he wanted to talk about it with Daddy Brendan, he couldn't. There was the always lingering fear Daddy would grow tired of him if he kept having problems instead of being his perfect boy, but it was more than that. The unrest inside him simmered like a boiling pot. Once you took the lid off, it would boil over, and there was no putting it back. Maybe this sadness, this sense of frustration and anger would go away again, but once he talked about it, that was it. Then it would always be there.

No, this would pass. It had to.

BRENDAN WORRIED ABOUT RAF. He'd been down the last few weeks, and ever since his talk with the principal, it had gotten even worse. It had nothing to do with their relationship, that much he was convinced of. They were doing better than ever together, growing closer by the day. The sex was phenomenal, and the connection between them just as special. Raf trusted Brendan completely, and he'd proven to be open to pretty much anything.

No, it had to do with his job. Or maybe with himself. Raf's usual spark was missing. It was there, but it was like his light had been dimmed somehow, like his star shone a little less bright. He'd asked Raf about school, if anything more had happened. Raf had assured him everything was fine, and yet Brendan worried.

He was waiting for Raf to come home from a team-building event when his phone rang. He checked the caller ID. Huh, that was unexpected.

"Rhys," he said as he picked up. "Is everything okay?"

"Raf isn't home, right?" Rhys asked, and Brendan's worry increased tenfold with that simple question.

"No, I'm not expecting him back for another half hour or so."

"Good. I'm worried about him, and I wanted to check in with you."

Brendan blew out a slow breath. "I'm worried too. Everything at work seems to be okay, or so he says, but he's different."

"Yeah, he is. He's too subdued, almost a little lethargic at times."

Well, he hadn't imagined it, then. At least that was a

reassurance, but Brendan's heart grew heavier. "Do you have any idea what it could be?"

Rhys breathed quietly for a while before he answered. "Raf told me you know he has ADHD."

"I do, and I'm doing my best to read up on it and understand it and him better."

"I'm glad to hear that, though from what I heard about you, I had expected nothing else. Has he told you about his father as well?"

"He has. I know things were hard for him growing up."

Rhys let out a deep sigh. "They were. I didn't spend a lot of time at his house because it was like stepping into a fridge, but his father was awful. He even had the guts one time to set me as an example to Raf because I'd won some stupid sportsmanship award in sixth grade. His father wasn't merely a homophobe but a perfection-demanding asshole as well. Raf was never accepted for who he was, neither for being gay or for his ADHD. And his mom never said a damn thing, not until he tried to kick Raf out for being gay."

Brendan forced down the anger that bubbled up inside him. He'd known all this, but to hear it confirmed by Rhys pissed him off all over again. None of this was Rhys's fault—on the contrary—so there was no reason to take it out on him.

"Raf told me your parents were wonderful, and I've been blessed with loving and supporting parents as well, so this makes me so angry and sad for him. He deserved so much better."

"It damaged him. I've always been amazed he managed to keep that inner joy, that it wasn't forced out of him."

"Except now it seems he lost it. Why now? What happened? Is it because of me? Of us?"

His heart clenched painfully at the thought. Could it be he was making things worse? Was their Daddy-boy dynamic harmful to Raf? It seemed too cruel to even consider.

"I don't think so. I think it's because of what happened at school, with that little kid. The way he talked about it felt to me as if it had triggered something in him."

Brendan considered it. "Did he ever talk to someone about his youth? Like therapy?"

"No. I suggested it a few times when he'd just left home, but he said he was fine...and in his defense, he did seem fine."

The guilt in Rhys's voice was easy to spot. "That's not on you, Rhys. You did an amazing job taking care of him all those years. I don't mean to sound condescending, but it's truly impressive, considering your age."

Rhys chuckled. "Thank you. No offense taken at all. Ford calls me an old soul. He says I was born mid-life or some crap."

"You're lucky with him as a mentor. He's not only a great Dom but a good man."

"He is." Rhys's voice grew serious. "He's been checking in a lot with me to make sure I'm okay."

"As I said, a good man. So are you? Okay, I mean? "

Rhys let out a frustrated sigh. "I guess. It's hard, grieving. You think you're finally getting better, that you're through the worst, and then it hits you all over again."

"I can't even imagine, especially since he died so young and unexpectedly. Did Raf tell you I knew your dad?"

Rhys made a sound of surprise. "No. How? From a club?"

"Yeah, but he also custom-built the changing table in my little-room. He did a phenomenal job."

"That's..." Rhys's voice sounded a little choked. "I'd love to see it sometime. I mean, Raf showed me the room once, but I didn't really pay attention."

Considering the circumstances, that made total sense to Brendan. "You're welcome anytime, Rhys. I really liked your dad. And Cornell too," he couldn't resist adding.

Rhys chuckled. "I guess Raf told you, huh?"

Brendan didn't want to throw his boy under the bus, but surely being open would work better for everyone? "He did, but I won't tell anyone. And I impressed upon Raf he shouldn't spill it either."

"Oh, he won't. He's known for years and never told a soul."

"*Years*?"

Rhys laughed again. "Apparently, I'm really loyal and stubborn. Or plain stupid. Haven't made up my mind which of the two yet."

Brendan smiled. "Love makes you stupid sometimes." Then he sobered. "So what do you suggest I do about Raf? Do I confront him?"

Rhys made a noncommittal sound. "One of the consequences of the damage his father has inflicted is that Raf is horribly afraid of disappointing people. It took him a long time to truly let his guard down with me."

Brendan understood what Rhys wasn't saying. "He may not be there with me yet. You're saying he may be scared to show me what's going on with him out of fear of disappointing me."

"Yeah, exactly. He loves you, Brendan. I've never seen him like this. Every time he even mentions you, his whole face lights up. But it also means he's scared to lose you, scared to mess things up. His father made him feel like nothing he did was ever good enough and that no matter how hard he tried, he'd always fuck up in the end. He's waiting for it to go wrong, waiting for you to grow frustrated with him just like everyone else."

He'd done that last time, Brendan realized. When Brendan had been an ass and retreated, Raf tried to be at his best behavior, to ensure he did whatever he could to make Brendan happy with him. It hurt deep inside that his boy had been so deeply wounded.

"I don't know how to handle this, let alone fix this, but I will," he promised Rhys. "I love him more than anything, and I'll make sure he's okay. You go take care of yourself."

"Thank you. That's a big relief. And I will. My next challenge is to convince Cornell he needs to stay at my place to recover."

Brendan chuckled. "Good luck with that. I can only hope he's not as stubborn as you."

17

Tucked against his Daddy's chest with a binkie in his mouth and fidgeting with his little blankie, Raf felt the tension seep out of his body. He'd come home from work bone-tired with his head spinning and buzzing. There had been many days like this lately. Too many.

Dolores had called him out today on forgetting to organize the classroom's library, which he'd promised to do and had forgotten for weeks now. Every time he'd thought of it or had remembered to check his little notebook, it had been at the wrong time, and in the end, he'd never gotten around to it. She'd been right to confront him, and that was what hurt most.

He was slipping, even though he tried harder than he ever had in his life and was taking his meds and everything. Hell, he was even sleeping better than ever before and eating healthy, thanks to Daddy Brendan. And still, he was messing up on a daily basis now, both at work and with Daddy and Rhys.

He'd forgotten to call Rhys again, and so his friend had

called him. He'd been understanding as he always was, but Raf had heard the layer of frustration. Even when he was struggling so hard himself, Rhys still had to make allowances for Raf.

His dad had been right. He was a fuckup, and that voice in his head that told him it was only a matter of time before Daddy Brendan would find out as well got stronger every day. Every time he messed up, it grew in volume and intensity. For so long, he'd been determined to beat it, to prove him wrong, but lately, he'd grown more and more convinced his dad had been right all along. He was still an asshole for pointing it out the way he had, but Raf couldn't deny the man had had a point.

"What are you thinking about so hard, baby boy?" Daddy Brendan said, his voice soft as his index finger stroked Raf's forehead. "You have your worry-frown. I don't like seeing that on you, baby boy. Is there something you want to tell Daddy?"

It was a rhetorical question because Raf wasn't allowed to talk during binkie-lap time, but Daddy Brendan would ask again after. And what was Raf supposed to say? Lie that everything was fine when it wasn't? But he couldn't tell him the truth either, not when he needed him as much as he did, when his heart couldn't even bear the thought of being without him.

"Your frown is getting deeper. What's going on, baby boy?"

There was an edge to Daddy's voice, his concern reaching deep inside Raf. Should he tell him? No, he couldn't. Daddy would dump him. No one wanted to be with a fuckup like him.

"Raf, I need you to listen to me." Daddy's voice got even more intense, and his eyes were drilling into Raf's. "I can see something's troubling you, and if you're not ready to talk, I will respect that. But if you're not telling me because you're scared of how I will react, then please know that whatever it is that's bothering you, we can deal with it. I love you, baby boy, and nothing you say can change that."

Yeah, right. Raf stilled as that thought hit him. He looked at Daddy's eyes, filled with so much love and concern. Everything Daddy did showed how much he cared for Raf, and yet Raf felt deep inside that he couldn't truly mean it. His love had to have boundaries. Like, if he found out how much of a mess Raf was on the inside, he'd stop loving him...right?

Hesitantly, he reached for his binkie and pulled it out of his mouth. When Daddy Brendan didn't say anything about him breaking the rules, Raf took a deep breath. "I'm scared."

There, that was said. It was a beginning, right?

Daddy pulled him closer, his face showing nothing but love. "There's nothing to be scared of, baby boy. You're not alone. You've got me, and you have Rhys, no matter what."

Rhys. Rhys had never given up on him either, and he'd seen Raf on some really bad days. Weeks, if you wanted to get literal. He'd had periods like this before, when the darkness seemed to creep into his brain more than usual, when he couldn't keep up the pretense that everything was fine. And Rhys had understood and had still been there. He had still loved him. That was real love. Something clicked inside Raf, something he'd never understood before.

"You love me," he said slowly.

Daddy Brendan didn't laugh at that obvious statement. "Very much."

"Love means you love someone, no matter what."

"Yes. Love is unconditional, baby boy. If someone only

loves you if you're good or if you do what they tell you, that's not love."

How could words heal and hurt at the same time? It was hard to breathe when this hit so deep, stabbing him through his heart while wrapping around him like a soft scarf at the same time. Brendan loved him, really loved him. That hit home now, and it made him feel like he could fly. But at the same time there was that deep cut, that ice-cold stab that he allowed fully in for the first time.

"I don't think my parents love me. They never did."

The words hung heavy, accusing, but Raf refused to take them back. It was the truth, no matter how much it hurt.

"Oh, baby boy," Daddy whispered, his voice full of emotions.

Raf looked at him, the pain in his eyes that mirrored Raf's own hurt. This man loved him, and how lucky was he that he'd found him, that they had found each other. But it didn't negate the pain inside him that filled him now with a new intensity.

"I've never allowed myself to feel that, let alone say that. It feels wrong to even think it, but I can't deny it any longer."

Daddy didn't say anything but just held him, those big arms tight. Raf fidgeted with his blankie, his thoughts racing through his head. It felt like a tornado, a thunderstorm with dark clouds and strong winds that left him reeling. Why did they not love him? What was wrong with him that they'd never accepted him?

No, the fault was with them. Hadn't Daddy said that as well weeks ago? This was on them, not on him. Every kid was worthy of love, and he was no exception. Besides, not loving someone because they were gay or had a limitation or whatever you wanted to call his ADHD, that was not okay. You couldn't blame him because he'd chosen neither.

It was who he was, and if his parents couldn't love him because of that, that was on them.

But god, it hurt. It hurt more deeply than anything he'd ever felt before, and when he lifted a tired hand to rub his eyes, he discovered he was crying. For some reason, that did him in. He'd held back from feeling this for so long, but now he couldn't hold back the flood anymore. He opened the gates in his mind, in his soul, and let the water in, hoping he wouldn't drown.

No, he wouldn't because Daddy was his anchor, his life vest. He would never let Raf drown. And with that knowledge, Raf let go and surrendered to the grief and pain inside him.

BRENDAN COULD IMAGINE nothing worse than having to watch his boy fall apart. This wasn't a mere crying fit. This was years and years of neglected pain coming out with a force that scared Brendan a little. Heavy sobs wracked Raf's body, and his pretty face had turned into a red, swollen, blubbery mess. His voice was hoarse from crying—these deep, long wails that seemed to originate in his soul. Every single one hurt Brendan in the depths of his heart. And every single one consolidated his love for him.

How he loved him. And how he wanted to beat the living crap out of Raf's dad. It wasn't an option nor a solution, but god, it would be satisfying. Maybe that was the worst thing, knowing the pain had already been inflicted and there was nothing he could do about it. He hadn't been there when it happened, and he couldn't even stop it now. All he could do was be there and hold him. Love him.

That was becoming clearer and clearer, how much love

Raf needed. He deserved a lifetime of being pampered and spoiled, of being made to feel like he was the brightest star in the universe, the very center of Brendan's world, just to make up for his youth.

It was impossible for Brendan to understand that this sweet, funny, sparkling boy had not been loved. How could you not love him? How could you not see all the good in him? He was their son, their child. How could parents justify rejecting their own kids? Brendan had heard it so many times before, and he'd never understood.

Finally, after what must've been at least an hour, Raf calmed down. He hung against Brendan, exhausted.

"How about we take a nap together, baby boy?"

Raf's eyes were almost shut from crying so much. "I feel so messy. Dirty."

Brendan wasn't sure if he meant that literally or emotionally, but he might have a solution for both. "So we'll take a bath together first. Let Daddy take care of you, baby boy."

Raf nodded tiredly, and Brendan pressed a kiss on his forehead, which was clammy with sweat. He rolled them both off the couch, then picked Raf up. His boy immediately wrapped his arms and legs around him, putting his head on Brendan's shoulder. "That's it, baby boy. Lean on Daddy."

He carried him up, managing to hold on to him, even when he ran the bath, throwing in some of Raf's favorite bubble bath. They'd both smell like bubblegum for a week, but it was a price Brendan was more than willing to pay.

He carried him into the playroom, where he put him down on the changing table. Raf was limp as Brendan undressed him, not saying anything but following his moves with heavy eyes. Brendan let him rest there for a minute as he undressed, then picked him back up and carried him into the bathroom.

He gently lowered him into the bathtub first, not daring to step in holding him, too scared he would slip and fall, hurting them both. Once Raf was seated, Brendan got in behind him, grateful all over again for installing that gigantic bathtub. Best investment ever, aside from his playroom.

As soon as he was seated, Raf scooted up so he could lean against him, his back pressed against Brendan's chest. Because of their difference in size, Raf liked to sit on his lap in the tub rather than between his legs, which would bring him too close to the waterline. He usually liked to tease Brendan by squirming on his lap, rubbing that sweet, round butt against Brendan's cock. This time, he sat quietly.

"I'm so tired," Raf whispered after a while, his voice scratchy. "Not just tired in my body, but on the inside. In my head, in my heart, everything. It's as if everything is taking so much more effort."

"I know it's been hard for you. I see how tired you are when you come home every day."

"Is it supposed to be this hard? Life, I mean? Or having a job? Because I've been there for weeks now, and it's not getting any better. I'm not getting any better at it either."

Brendan carefully weighed his words, knowing how vulnerable Raf was right now. "The transition into a full-time working life isn't easy. Lots of young adults struggle. And you've had a lot to deal with."

Raf tilted his head, meeting his eyes. "Not more than others, and they seem to manage. Just look at Rhys. He just lost his dad, and he's killing it at work."

Brendan wanted to tell him not to compare himself with

anyone else, but hadn't he just done the same by stating lots of young adults struggle with this? It was such a catch-22. "Rhys is a different person with a completely different set of circumstances and a different job. I don't think the comparison is fair."

"Because of my ADHD," Raf said with a sigh.

"Partially, but also because Rhys had a different upbringing than you did. He's grieving a father who loved him deeply and made sure Rhys knew. You're grieving a father who never accepted you for who you were. That's a shaky foundation to build your life on."

Raf was quiet for a while, surprisingly calm as he sat on Brendan's lap. Usually, Brendan had to play games with him or distract him with something so he wouldn't fidget all the time. He was probably so worn out from his crying spell he was too tired to even be restless.

"So where does that leave me? It's not like I can change the past. Does that mean I'm fucked up for life?"

For a fraction of a second, Brendan considered letting the F-bomb go, but more than anything, Raf needed that stability right now. He needed all the structure and rules Brendan could give him.

He lifted his arm and quickly twisted Raf's nipple.

"Ouch!" Raf let out, sounding annoyed and a little miffed. "That hurt, Daddy."

"That was the intention. Language, Raphael, and don't let me have to warn you again."

After a second or two, Raf's body released its tension. "Sorry, Daddy," his boy said, and Brendan knew he'd gotten it right.

"But to answer your question, no, baby boy, you're not messed up for life. As much as I hate to say it, a lot of people grow up without parental love and support, and they do just fine. I think the key is to talk about it, to find someone who can help you process this."

After what Rhys had told him about Raf rejecting therapy years ago, he hoped he'd hit the right tone and hadn't pushed too hard.

"You mean therapy."

"Yes. I think that with all the changes in your life and this deep realization you had about your upbringing, therapy could be helpful to you to process."

Again, Raf took his time answering, but Brendan set quietly, content to wait.

"I don't like therapists," Raf said with a slight tremble in his voice.

Of course. Brendan wanted to slap himself for not considering that option. "Did your parents ever take you to a therapist when you were small?"

"Yes." Raf's voice was barely more than a whisper. "But I don't think he was a *real* therapist. He was a member of the church my parents went to at the time, and my father hired him to help me develop healthy masculinity. That's what they called it: healthy masculinity. It was code for being straight, of course."

Conversion therapy. If there was one topic that got Brendan's blood boiling, it was that one. How much emotional damage had been done to the LGBT community in the name of therapy, in the name of God? It was inconceivable that in this day and age, people still didn't understand that you couldn't talk someone into being straight, let alone scare them or force them. How could people not see that?

"I'm so sorry. Did they hurt you?"

It was the best he could think of to ask. He didn't want to force Raf into sharing even more emotional trauma, not after the meltdown he just had, but he had to ask to ascertain the severity of what he'd been through.

"Not physically. It was a lot of Bible study and heavy talks. More indoctrination than anything else, or at least attempt at indoctrination. And I wasn't the only one. It was group therapy, so there was some strange comfort in that."

Brendan rested his chin on Raf's head. "How long did that last?"

Raf let out a deep sigh. "Three years. From when I was ten until my thirteenth birthday, and then the so-called counselor got fired by the church. I never found out why, but rumors were that he had been inappropriate with some women he counseled."

"I can understand why an experience like that would make you reluctant about therapy, but I swear we'll find you a real therapist. A good one. One who has experience with the LGBT community and preferably also with ADHD. I promise I will come with you the first few times to make sure it's a good fit."

Raf pushed against his arms, and Brendan let go of him, surprised when the boy turned around on his lap and sat down facing him. "You really want this."

"Therapy? It's your choice, baby boy, like everything else, but I think you could benefit from it. I've been worried about you, you know. I knew something was going on."

Raf lowered his eyes. "I was so scared to tell you."

Brendan had no trouble understanding why now. "You were afraid that if you told me about the turmoil inside your head, I would leave you."

Raf bit his lip as he peeked at Brendan from underneath his lashes. "I have a hard time believing you really love me, no matter what. With my head, I know you do, but my heart struggles with grasping it."

Brendan cupped his cheek, tilting his head up, and met his eyes. "Baby boy, that's completely understandable, and I would never get upset with you over that. I hope you'll allow me to prove to you over time how much I love you and that love is real and not contingent on you behaving a certain way."

Raf nodded. "I love you, Daddy. Thank you for being patient with me."

"It's my pleasure. Please, if there's anything I can do for you, just ask me. You know there's nothing I wouldn't do to make you feel better."

Raf studied him for a few seconds more. "Daddy, will you make love to me?"

18

Raf closed his eyes as Daddy Brendan patted him dry with a towel. Daddy had these big, fluffy towels that were so soft on your skin. Quite the contrast with the thin, scratchy once he used in his apartment. Not that he'd been there recently.

Everywhere he dried Raf off, Daddy peppered him with soft kisses, setting his skin on fire. His back was completely dry now, and Daddy stepped behind him, pulling him close against him to start on the front. Raf loved the slight scratch of Daddy's chest hairs against his back. It always reminded him of how different they were and yet how perfectly they fit together.

Daddy blew a hot breath over his ear, making him shiver, as his hands were busy rubbing his chest dry. Two strong fingers caught his right nipple, rubbing it tenderly and rolling it between them until it was hard and aching for more. Liquid heat pooled in his belly, but he was in no rush at all.

His left nipple got the same treatment, and then Daddy dragged the towel slowly down. There was no happy trail to follow. He kept himself shaved completely. He loved how smooth it made his skin feel, and since he didn't have much body hair to begin with, it was an easy task. Daddy loved it too, always commenting on how soft Raf's skin was and how much he loved to kiss it, lick it, suck it. God, Daddy's mouth. It was an instrument of pleasure as well as torture.

A gentle hand wrapped the towel around his cock, thoroughly drying it off before moving along to his balls, already heavy. Daddy left no inch of his body untouched, and Raf sagged against him, leaning on his strength in every way.

"My beautiful boy," Daddy whispered in his ear, his voice low with want. "You are so perfect for me, my precious baby boy."

He *felt* perfect in moments like this, when his body was played like an expensive instrument, expertly brought to the height of its existence by a talented master. Sex had always been stressful for him, full of self-doubt and him going into his head, questioning what he was supposed to do. With Daddy Brendan, he never had to wonder. All he had to do was obey Daddy.

Daddy sunk to his knees, his hard cock dragging a wet trail down Raf's back and leg. He smiled. He'd have to shower again after, but that was the price he was more than willing to pay. His legs were dabbed dry, and then Daddy made him lift his feet one by one, making Raf giggle as he tickled his toes.

"There," Daddy said, satisfaction dripping from his voice. "That's better."

As warm and fluid as his body felt, it also felt empty inside. It was a state he had learned to recognize, to live with. The only time it was ever gone was when Daddy was buried inside him. There was nothing he loved more than the sensation of that fat cock splitting him wide open.

Daddy let go of him, though he kept a hand on his shoulder as he walked around Raf and stood in front of him. Raf looked up, meeting Daddy's eyes, which were blazing with love as well as desire. His eyes were dark, the pupils blown.

Daddy grabbed his neck and pulled him close. He had to lean in as Raf stood on his tippy toes to meet his mouth, which was greedy and impatient. His hot, slick tongue pushed against Raf's, and he let it, welcoming him in. He kissed him back with all he had, needing so much more.

Apparently the position was uncomfortable for Daddy as well because after only a few beats, he reached for Raf's hips and lifted him up. Raf wrapped his legs around Daddy's waist, happy to plaster himself against him and feel closer to him still.

Daddy trailed his mouth from Raf's lips to his cheek, nibbling on his earlobe before nuzzling his neck. His beard scratched against his sensitive skin, giving him goose bumps. Then Daddy's lips found that tender, hollow spot at the base of his throat and sucked. The pressure on his skin shot straight to Raf's cock, making him even harder.

Daddy was leaving his mark, and that shouldn't be as hot and sexy as it was, but Raf loved seeing the remnants of Daddy's claim on him the next day. A soft groan fell from his lips, causing Daddy to suck even harder.

"Mark me, Daddy," he heard himself say.

He wanted to be reminded that he was loved now. That he was safe. That he was fully accepted the way he was.

"Everywhere," Daddy promised him, and the words sent a thrill through Raf. True to his words, Daddy marked two other spots on his throat and shoulder, leaving hickeys so perfect they made Raf's stomach go weak.

"Let's move this to the bedroom," Daddy said.

He didn't wait for Raf to respond but carried him to the master bedroom, slowly lowering him onto the big bed. Raf stretched out, putting his body on full display for Daddy, who crawled beside him, his hands already reaching for Raf again.

Raf yelped when Daddy closed his hot mouth around his left nipple, his tongue teasing the little bud until it responded by becoming hard. Daddy smiled against his skin, then gently clamped his teeth around it and pulled. God. Raf clenched his eyes shut, his back arching as he leaned into Daddy's mouth. It should hurt, but it didn't. Or maybe it did but in a good way.

Daddy's tongue came to play again, and then he started a mad sequence of licking and sucking and scraping and biting and kissing and even twisting in a way that made Raf's nipples the very erotic center of his body. It was like all his nerves had connected there somehow, and every touch now made his heart speed up, his blood pump faster, his skin grow clammy, and his balls so hard they were throbbing.

"Daddy, too much," he protested, his voice breaking. "I can't take it anymore."

Daddy merely smiled at him. "You'll take whatever I give you, baby boy. I'm gonna make you fly higher than you've ever done before."

Raf arched his back even more when Daddy renewed his nipple play, then pulled back again when it got too much. But Daddy was unrelenting, driving him higher and higher until Raf was squirming, groaning, begging for mercy.

"Daddy, please. Please. It's too much."

Daddy lifted his head and looked at him, his lips still wet and slightly swollen. "You have no idea what it does to me to hear you beg."

He pushed himself up, then grabbed Raf's waist and turned him on his stomach. Raf let himself be manhandled, the sensation of Daddy's strong hands putting him exactly the way he wanted him always a turn-on. He obediently spread his legs when Daddy nudged them wider and pushed his upper body down low the way Daddy wanted him until he was laid out like a present for him, his ass wide open.

He felt Daddy's hot breath first, teasing his ass cheeks, his hole, which fluttered in response. He knew what was coming. Daddy had never made it a secret of how much he loved rimming Raf, and yet every time he eagerly anticipated the onslaught on his system, which was equal parts torture and pleasure.

Daddy rubbed his beard over Raf's ass cheeks, making him giggle. "That tickles, Daddy."

"I love your laugh," was the reply, and Raf put both his hands on Daddy's head in affection. Well, maybe also because he wanted him to hurry up a little. After all, his mouth was inches away from Raf's hole and his dick, and both of them surely could use some loving attention.

Daddy laughed. "You know better, baby boy. We're not on your schedule. I set the pace."

Yeah, yeah, he knew all right. Whenever he tried to hurry Daddy up, it only backfired on him. "Sorry, Daddy," he said. because that age-old adage was still true: you caught more flies with honey than with vinegar.

He was rewarded with a soft kiss on his hole, and he shivered. Then Daddy's tongue came out to taste him, and Raf fisted the sheets with both hands, crumpling them. Daddy licked around his rim, then kissed it, sucked it, and licked it again until it softened under his ministrations. Raf's body gave way, and when Daddy's tongue slipped inside him, there was no resistance left.

He loved being worked open like this. His hips rolled backward, seeking friction against Daddy's tongue, his mouth. His fingers tightened on Daddy's head as Daddy slid his hands down his body, rubbing him, caressing his skin with soft touches. Raf's cock pressed hard against the soft sheets, wetting them with precum. It was hard to keep his eyes open as they kept fluttering closed, his mind signaling it was on overload with all the sensations Daddy evoked in him.

He was stabbing Raf's hole now with his tongue, fucking it with slow, deep movements, still softening and opening him wide for what was to come. Raf thought of Daddy's casual remarks before, about maybe wanting to try fisting. He'd never done anything remotely like it but was definitely interested now. Well, not *now* now, but the next time. Whenever Daddy thought he would be ready for it.

Kisses rained down on his ass cheeks as Daddy moved from his hole to the surrounding skin, nibbling and tasting him wherever he could. It ignited a fire in Raf, an inferno of desire that had started in his balls and cock, but that was now raging throughout his body. How much more of this could he take?

He thrust back against Daddy Brendan, desperate for more. Daddy rolled on top of him, covering Raf's much smaller body with his bigger one. A mighty tremor barreled through Raf when their bodies slid together. His fingers dug even deeper into the mattress, and Daddy's hands slipped around him, his nails scratching over Raf's skin, which was already so sensitive.

He rocked backward again, harder, needing so much

more than what Daddy was giving him right now. "Daddy," he pleaded. "Daddy, please. I need you."

Daddy pressed open-mouthed kisses to his neck, his shoulders. "I'm gonna make you feel so good, baby boy. Stay with me now."

His right hand moved from underneath Raf, his fingers wiggling as if searching for something. The lube. With one hand, Daddy managed to open it and spread some on his fingers. He wrestled his hand between them, finding Raf's ass still wide open for him. Two fingers plunged deep inside him, and Raf keened. It was too good and yet not nearly enough.

Luckily, Daddy seemed to be more inclined to hurry as well, fingering Raf's ass open with deep thrusts and scissoring moves that left him panting. His body obeyed every little touch from his Daddy, wanting to please him more than anything. His abdomen curled, warmth spreading as the fire inside him roared even higher.

Two fingers became three. Would Daddy go for four or finally put that glorious dick inside him? Then four fingers pushed against him. He exhaled, relaxed, then bore down. It stung, but four fingers sunk inside him.

"My perfect baby boy," Daddy said, his voice so full of content and praise Raf felt it in his soul. "You'll take my whole hand one day, won't you?"

Yes, he would. No doubt about it. But not right now.

"Daddy," he groaned. "More, Daddy."

Daddy's hand had been still inside him, but then he carefully thrust those four fingers. God, it burned. It stung, tendrils of pain licking his ass on the inside. But there was pleasure too, the fire that had been stoked up so high, overtaking the pain, obliterating it. Pain and pleasure became one as Daddy used those four big fingers to work him wide open.

He'd never done it this way, lying on his stomach, unable to meet Daddy's eyes. On one hand, he missed seeing Daddy's eyes on him, but on the other hand, it felt so much dirtier, perfect in a way he'd never expected. Even though Daddy was, as always, focused on Raf's pleasure, it felt like he was using him too. And Raf *liked* that feeling, liked the fact that he had nothing to say in this, even though he knew that one word would stop it all.

One second, four fingers were buried to the hilt inside him, and the next, Daddy's fat cockhead pushed against him. It slid in with ease, worked open as he was, and Raf welcomed him. Daddy laid himself on top of him, the fur of his chest hair tickling Raf's skin as he slid all the way inside.

He didn't wait for Raf to adjust but moved with slow, almost gentle strokes that made Raf shiver and shake. He let go of the sheets and folded his arms, putting his hand on top of it. His legs were still spread wide, and Daddy had found a spot between them, resting on top of him in a way that made Raf feel protected and ravished at the same time.

Daddy gently bit his earlobe. "I'm gonna take my time with you. Drive you crazy until you'll be begging to come."

Raf swallowed. "If I beg now, can we move things along?"

Daddy pulled out his cock almost entirely, then slid back in with a move that made Raf feel every inch of his length and girth. That would be a no, then. Not that he had expected anything else.

Their bodies were pressed so closely together, Daddy's hips rolling and flexing as he drove deep into Raf over and over again, that Raf could feel Daddy's heart beat against his back. He turned his head sideways, and Daddy pressed his cheek against his. They were linked in every way, two bodies becoming one, two souls merging.

The tightness in Raf's chest loosened, as well as the tension in his muscles, until he was nothing but a pliant body, willing to do whatever his Daddy asked him to. His mind let go of all the worries, all the sadness and grief until there was nothing left but this. Nothing but Daddy filling him, loving him, making him climb higher and higher until the flames engulfed him.

And when he finally fell, it was after rising higher than he'd ever thought possible, every cell in his body exploding with his orgasm. This was what love felt like, he thought before crashing into a dead sleep.

19

Things had never been better between him and his boy, and even though Raf's mental state hadn't changed, they were closer than ever. Brendan had carefully brought up the subject of therapy a few times, and when Raf hadn't balked, he'd inquired to find a good therapist.

Jacki had recommended someone she'd had good experiences with, and since he trusted her more than anyone else, he'd booked an appointment for Raf in two weeks. Obviously, he would be going with him. No way was he sending his boy off to someone he didn't know and hadn't met personally. Not after what had happened to him as a teen.

His work was busy as well. His team had been busting their asses, trying to close a big deal with a company that flipped houses. Just before he left for home, Brendan had heard they'd gotten the contract, and he was in the mood to celebrate.

Raf was already home when he got there, playing games

on the Xbox. "Hi, Daddy." The genuine smile on his face every time he saw Brendan did something to him inside.

"Hi, baby boy. How was your day?" he asked as he bent and pressed a kiss on those soft lips.

"I had a really good day at work. Dolores said I was on top of everything this week and didn't forget a single thing. She said she would tell the principal as well."

"That's amazing, baby boy. I'm so proud of you."

"How was your day, Daddy?"

Brendan lowered himself onto the couch next to Raf. "I had a really good day as well. We closed on a deal we'd worked on for weeks, and I'm elated we got the contract. It's a long-term contract for a hefty sum, so this means a lot for my company."

Raf's eyes widened. "Congratulations, Daddy. I'm so happy for you. I know how hard you worked on this."

Brendan smiled at him. "I'm in the mood to celebrate. How about we go out for a nice dinner?"

Raf had been so tired they'd stayed inside a lot. They'd hung out at Rhys's house a few times, but other than that, they'd barely gone out. Focusing on his job took most of Raf's energy, and Brendan didn't want to do anything that could risk his performance.

Raf nodded instantly. "That sounds good, Daddy. Do I need to dress up?"

Most of Raf's clothes had found their way into Brendan's closet in the master bedroom. He wasn't sure when was the last time Raf had been in his own apartment, but it had to be weeks ago. They only stopped in once a week to pick up his mail, and that was it. His room only held his furniture now. Most of his personal possessions had already found a spot somewhere in Brendan's house.

"You know what? Let's dress up a little. I'd love to see you in something nice," Brendan decided.

Raf's face lit up. "I'm on it."

Brendan quickly refreshed himself, then put on a nice dress shirt, a pair of dark gray slacks, and his good shoes. He'd trimmed his beard two days ago, so all he needed to do was work the edges a little to look more than presentable.

Meanwhile, Raf had taken over the guest bedroom, and all kinds of noises came from that bathroom, which made him smile. When Raf came downstairs, Brendan whistled. "Baby boy, you look amazing. Let me have a good look at you."

Raf immediately spun around for him, showing off the tight, black pants that hugged every curve of his body. He'd combined it with a thin, multicolored, shimmery top that sparkled whenever he moved. A pair of what looked to be brand-new Converse in bright pink completed his outfit.

"I put on a little makeup."

Brendan had no trouble spotting the hesitancy in his voice. He sent him a warm smile. "Let me see."

He'd put something sparkly on his eyelids, and a thin layer of eyeliner or something brought out the color of his eyes. His lips were shimmery as well, and Brendan thought he'd never looked sexier. Or kissable, though that would certainly ruin those perfect lips.

"You are gorgeous, baby boy. Absolutely beautiful. I'm proud to have you on my arm tonight."

Raf beamed, and that smile stayed on his face as they got into the car and drove over to the restaurant Brendan had called quickly to make a reservation. There was no wait, and the hostess led them to a lovely table in the back of the restaurant where they had more privacy than Brendan had counted on. It was perfect.

They chatted until their waiter arrived, a college-aged guy who gave them a friendly smile. "Hi, I'm Jason and I'll be taking care of you tonight. Tonight's specials are line-caught, pan-seared tuna with grilled asparagus, wild mushrooms, rice noodles, and a lime-cilantro dressing, or a vegetarian homemade risotto with six different wild mushrooms in a creamy lemon sauce with grilled winter vegetables."

Brendan's mouth watered at the descriptions.

"Can I start you off with something to drink?" Jason asked.

Raf looked at him. "Can I have a glass of wine, Daddy?"

They both froze at that habitual title, but Jason didn't even blink. Brendan cleared his throat. "Of course."

"Can I have a glass of sweet white wine, please?" Raf ordered.

Jason's smile was nothing but friendly and professional. "Sure, but I'd like to see some ID, please."

Once Raf had shown him his driver's license, Jason scribbled the order on his little notepad. "And for you, sir?"

"I'll have seltzer with lemon, please. Thank you."

"Absolutely. I'll be right back with your drinks, but please take your time to look over the menu."

As soon as Jason was gone, Raf snickered. "Sorry, Daddy. It's become such a habit I didn't even think about it."

Brendan smiled back. "I don't mind. You can call me Daddy whenever you want. The choice is yours. I've told you before I don't care what people think. So do whatever makes you comfortable."

Raf cocked his head. "The server didn't even look surprised."

"That's because he probably thought you were my son."

Raf's eyes widened. "Really? That's..."

"Well, it's a logical assumption, don't you think? What he

sees is an older guy with a young man, a young man who calls him Daddy. Trust me, a Daddy-boy relationship isn't the first thing people think of in a situation like that."

"When you put it like that, it makes sense. And that doesn't bother you either? That people think you're my real dad?"

Brendan leaned forward, resting with his arms on the table. "The question is if it bothers you."

Raf seemed to consider it, the scrunch at the top of his nose indicating he was thinking. "Maybe a little, but I want to take a page from your book and not be bothered by it."

Pride bloomed in Brendan's heart. "I'm proud of you, baby boy."

They looked over at the menu, and Brendan quickly made up his mind that the tuna special sounded delicious. But it seemed Raf had a much harder time choosing, fidgeting with the menu and flipping back and forth between the two pages.

"Having trouble?" Brendan asked.

Raf's eyes met him over the menu. "I can't choose. There's so much that looks good."

He was saying one thing, but the edge in his voice told Brendan there was something else going on as well. It was not so much tension as a hint of something else. Shame? Embarrassment? But what could Raf possibly be embarrassed about here?

He kept watching him until Raf put down the menu and send him a careful smile. "It's been a while since I had to make a choice like this."

Things clicked for Brendan. "Would you like Daddy to choose for you?"

Relief exploded over Raf's face. “Would you, Daddy? It's

hard for me to choose with so many choices, and I know you'll choose the perfect thing for me."

God, his heart. His poor, full, exploding heart. It was almost too much to feel, to bear, this heady sensation of loving and being loved this deeply. He reached for Raf's hand, lacing their fingers together. "It would be my pleasure."

When Jason came back with their drinks, his eyes fell to their joined hands, but other than a slight widening of his eyes, he never showed any reaction. Brendan couldn't help but be grateful for this generation of young people who seemed so much more open than many of his age.

"Have you guys come to a decision, or would you like a little more time to peruse the menu?" Jason asked.

"I would love to try that tuna special, and for him, I'd like the seasoned pork chops with the broccoli. Can we exchange the fries that come with it for the garlic mashed potatoes? And do you maybe have some applesauce on the side?"

"Absolutely. I'll get that order right in for you."

"Thank you, Daddy," Raf said when Jason had left again. "That sounds delicious."

"I know you love pork chops. And there's no way you're going to eat that broccoli without a little applesauce," Brendan said with a little chuckle. He knew his boy well by now.

Raf's glass of wine was empty within a few minutes, a rosy stain on his cheeks indicating the alcohol was affecting him. "I like this, Daddy. Going out with you, I mean."

"We could go to the club together sometime." He hadn't been back since he'd met Raf there, but the truth was he hadn't even missed it. How could he, when he had everything he wanted right across the table from him? "I would be proud to show you off as my boy."

At first, Raf smiled, but then his smile faltered. "What if I make a mistake again? I didn't really make a good impression the first time. Or the second and third. I think half the Doms must hate me."

His poor boy, still haunted by his failed experiments. "First of all, I doubt that. Master Ford really liked you, or so Rhys told me, and he would not tolerate anyone speaking badly about his protégé's best friend. Second, you did nothing wrong. Experimenting is part of our lifestyle. How else can we find out what we connect with?"

That seemed to appease Raf, and some of the tension left his face. "How did you discover you liked being a Daddy?"

"I saw a demonstration in a different club. They had what they called an open weekend, where outsiders could visit and attend several demonstrations of a wide variety of kinks. There were the usual suspects, like bondage, mild pain play, and some humiliation play, but there was also a Daddy with his little. It didn't draw a lot of attention, but from the moment I laid eyes on them, I was hooked. The way he took care of his boy, diapering him, then feeding him a bottle—it was everything I never knew I wanted."

"Same. Not the demonstration, but the fact that this is exactly what I wanted. How did you know it would be a good fit for me?"

Brendan leaned back in his chair, stretching his legs under the table. "It was the way you asked Rhys if he would make you a hot cocoa. Your voice changed from an adult into a boy, and it was clear to me how much you needed that care. Then when we did our little experiment and you fell asleep while sucking my thumb, well, let's just say I knew right there and then."

They were still chatting when the food arrived, and conversation flowed easily during the meal. Raf had asked for a second glass of wine, and Brendan had acquiesced, though he wasn't sure if it was a wise idea. He didn't want to get into an argument in front of Jason, however, but when Raf gobbled down that second glass as well, he wasn't happy with his decision.

When they got up after finishing and paying, Raf wavered a little, and Brendan's hand shot out and steadied him. "You okay, baby boy?"

"Yeah. Just a little tipsy."

Brendan frowned as they walked out, him holding Raf's arm just to be sure. "How can you be tipsy from two glasses of wine? Are you that much of a light weight?"

As soon as he had asked, he knew the answer. Dammit. He grabbed Raf's shoulder and turned him around. "It's your medication, isn't it? It interacts with alcohol."

Raf had never looked more guilty. "Yes," he whispered, pushing his bottom lip out. "It hits me much harder."

Brendan grabbed his chin, forcing him to meet his eyes. "That's something you should have told me, Raphael."

Oh, the guilt on Raf's face. Brendan had to tread lightly here. "I love you, baby boy, and we're not going to let this spoil such a lovely evening. We'll talk about this tomorrow, okay?"

"I'm sorry, Daddy. Please don't be angry with me."

It was a difficult position for him to be in. With any other boy, he would've flat-out told him he was angry and disappointed, but those words would cut Raf. On the other hand, he couldn't let something like this slide either. Raf had definitely crossed a line, and he needed to know.

Brendan would need time to figure out how best to handle this. But for now, reassuring his boy was more important.

He let go of his chin and pressed a kiss on his forehead. "I'm not angry with you. I love you, you know that. Don't fret over it, okay? We'll talk about it tomorrow."

All during the ride home, Raf kept stealing glances at him, that worried line etched on his forehead. Whenever he caught his stare, Brendan gave him a smile to reassure him. By the time they got home, Raf seemed to have relaxed a bit more.

They settled on the couch, and Brendan picked a movie for them to watch. His guess was that Raf would fall asleep soon, considering his alcohol intake, and he was right. Half an hour into *Love, Simon,* Raf was asleep, melted against him.

Brendan carried him up the stairs, laying him onto the bed. Raf half awoke when Brendan undressed him, stripping him down to his cute, pink boxers. "I love you, Daddy," he said, blinking. "You're the best Daddy ever. I'm sorry I got drunk."

Brendan smiled as he kissed him. "I love you too. You are the best boy ever. Now, go to sleep. Daddy's got you."

20

Raf plunked himself down on Rhys's couch and promptly regretted it. He winced as his ass reminded him that it wasn't a good idea to disobey Daddy Brendan. Even though he was wearing his diaper, it still hurt to sit down that hard.

Rhys lifted an eyebrow. "Sore ass?"

Raf leaned sideways to rub it, keeping his scowl to a minimum. He felt Daddy Brendan's eyes on him. "Yeah. Daddy spanked me this afternoon."

Rhys's mouth pulled up in a grin. "What did you do to deserve that?"

Raf rolled his eyes at his friend. Of course Rhys would take Daddy's side. He should've known. Though if he were honest, he'd deserved every slap of the spanking Daddy had given him and then some. "I didn't tell him how alcohol affected me and then got drunk on two glasses of wine yesterday when we went out for dinner."

Rhys rolled his eyes right back at him. "Dude. You deserved it."

Raf sent Daddy an apologetic look. "I know. It was stupid. But my ass hurts."

Rhys didn't seem impressed. "That should teach you not to keep things from your Daddy."

"Is it, like, a rule to something that you Doms stick together?" Raf complained, but Rhys merely grinned.

"How's Cornell doing?" Raf asked, desperately wanting to change the subject.

"I think he'll be released soon. Maybe even this week."

"Have you talked to him about staying with you?"

Rhys shifted his eyes. "Not yet."

"If he's going home soon, wouldn't now be, like, the right time for that?" Raf didn't understand what the problem was. Rhys could ask, right? Where was the harm? The worst thing that could happen was the man would say no.

"It's not quite that easy," Rhys mumbled.

"It never is," Daddy Brendan said, who seemed to understand what the problem was.

"How are you liking age play? Still a fan?" Rhys asked, and it was such a dumb question after how much Raf had shared with him that he recognized it for the same tactic he'd used before. Apparently, Rhys didn't want to talk about Cornell. Raf would respect that. He owed him that much, if not a hell of a lot more.

"I love it. Daddy keeps trying new things with me, and I love it all."

"What's your favorite?"

Raf shrugged. "That depends on how I feel. If I'm super stressed, I love playtime with the trains or cars. If my head is busy and won't quiet down, binkie-lap time with Daddy always helps. But I also love my bubble baths or the bottle or Daddy napping with me. And diapers, I love those too. I'm wearing one now."

The smile Rhys sent him was genuine. "I already spotted it. I'm so happy for you, for both of you. It took us a while to find out what your thing was, but I'm so glad we did."

Raf's insides flooded with gratitude. How lucky was he that he could talk about this with his best friend without him batting an eye or thinking he was deranged for not only wearing a diaper but loving it? "Me too. It's changed everything for me."

"I want to show you something," Rhys said. "Come with me for a sec."

Raf got up from the couch—moving more carefully this time—and followed Rhys to the big cabinet in the living room, where he pulled open a drawer. It held a bin, and when Rhys opened it, Raf gasped.

"You have toy cars? Since when?"

Rhys put a soft hand on his shoulder. "Since I know you're into this. I bought a play rug, too, and some other stuff. I want this house to be a safe space for you, Raf, so if you ever need to calm down or relax and your Daddy isn't there, you can always come here. Or if you just want to hang out."

Raf's eyes grew moist. "You'd be okay with me as a little?"

Rhys affectionately rubbed Raf's curls. "More than okay. I love you the way you are, buddy. And if you're happy playing with cars and wearing a diaper, that's more than fine with me. You can be yourself here."

Raf stepped into Rhys's arms and hugged him hard, burying his face against Rhys's chest. "Thank you for being my friend all those years. I wouldn't have survived without you."

Rhys kissed the top of his head. "You're welcome, but don't ever forget that you've been an equally good friend to me. I wouldn't be where I am without you. It goes both ways."

The warmth inside Raf spread out to every cell of his being. He really was lucky to have both Rhys and Daddy Brendan. "I'm so glad you and I never had sex."

Rhys let go of him, shaking with suppressed laughter. "Me too, but where the hell did that come from?"

"Oh, I was just thinking how happy I am to have you and Daddy, but if you and I had hooked up or whatever and the sex would've been bad, we wouldn't have been such good friends as we are now."

Rhys bellowed. "Why the hell would you assume the sex would've been bad?" he said in between fits of laughter.

"Because we kissed, and that sucked donkey balls!"

Raf didn't understand how he could not see that. They were like brothers, and the sexual chemistry between them was below freezing point.

"You guys kissed?" Daddy Brendan asked, and Raf rolled his eyes at Rhys, who was still laughing.

"Now you've made it awkward," Raf said, scowling.

"Dude, you're the one who brought up sex!"

Rhys had a point there, but whatever. Raf turned to Daddy Brendan. "We kissed once, back when we were like thirteen or so. Let's just say we decided we were better off as friends." He shot Rhys a quick look and then decided to get back at him a little. "He's not that great a kisser," he stage-whispered at Daddy Brendan, whose eyes danced with laughter.

"You little shit! You sucked at it as much as I did!" Rhys said.

Raf put his hands on his hips. "How come he can use cuss words, but when I do it, you punish me?" he asked Daddy Brendan, who merely shrugged.

"You're my boy, and he isn't, so what Rhys does is his own business."

"You Doms really do stick together," Raf muttered, but he wasn't really angry. He loved that his best friend and his Daddy got along so well.

Rhys rubbed his head again, then slung an arm around his shoulder as his eyes grew soft. "How are you feeling otherwise?"

Raf leaned against him. "The same. It's better, now that Daddy knows, but I'm still struggling. But Daddy found a therapist who looks promising, so we're going there next week to see if it's a good fit."

"I'm so proud of you for taking that step."

"I know you urged me to go years ago, and I'm sorry I didn't listen."

Rhys made him turn his head and face him. "You weren't ready yet. You are now. You'll get through this, Raf. You're so much stronger than you think."

His friend looked tired, traces of weeks of grieving and worrying over Cornell edged in his face. Raf rose to his tippy toes and pressed a soft kiss on Rhys's lips.

"So are you."

"How's my sweet boy feeling?" Daddy asked as he rubbed the baby powder he had just sprinkled on in with slow moves.

Raf let out a happy sigh. "I'm good, Daddy. Tired, but okay."

"I've got something special for you."

Raf's eyes widened. "Because I've been a good boy?"

"No, baby boy, because you *are* a sweet boy. You never have to earn my love, honey."

Why did Daddy always say things that made him cry? "What do you have for me?"

"Let me put on your new onesie, and then you'll find out."

Raf liked the new onesie, which had fire trucks on it. He still liked the one with the little monkeys best, but this one was cool too. When Daddy was done, he climbed off the changing table, immediately reaching for his hand.

"Where is it, Daddy?"

"Downstairs, on the dining table."

Raf wanted to run downstairs, but Daddy had warned him before about running inside the house, and the last thing he wanted now was to make Daddy upset with him, so he held back and managed to walk down calmly.

On the dining table was a flat, square, wrapped package that looked like a book. Daddy had tried reading to him before, but that hadn't worked for Raf, whose mind had trouble concentrating long enough to sit still and listen to a story. Had Daddy bought him another book to try? Or something to read himself?

"Can I open it?"

Daddy, who had followed him downstairs, slapped his butt in a playful way. "Of course. I hope you love it."

Raf tore the paper off right away and turned the book—because it *was* a book of some kind—over in his hands until he looked at the back. His breath caught in his lungs. It wasn't an ordinary book. It was a coloring book. He flipped through it, gasping when he saw the beautiful drawings of unicorns and butterflies and dragons and magical creatures, all waiting for him to color in.

"It's beautiful," he said softly.

"This goes with it," Daddy said, handing him another gift-wrapped package.

Raf made short work of the wrapping again, revealing the biggest box of colored pencils he'd ever seen. And they weren't the cheap ones either. He put them down on the table before flinging himself at Daddy, who caught him effortlessly, as always.

"Thank you so much, Daddy. It's perfect! Can I please go color now?"

Daddy kissed him first, a deep, hungry kiss that promised him more later. "Absolutely. I'm so happy you like it."

Like it? He *loved* it. How could he not? Minutes later, Raf sat installed at the table with his new coloring book and the pencils, starting on a gorgeous drawing of a momma dragon with her baby. His tongue peeked out between his lips as he colored as neat as he could.

"Don't forget to drink your juice, baby boy," Daddy said.

Raf reached for his sippy cup mindlessly, emptying it quickly "Done, Daddy."

He went straight back to coloring. He was almost done with the drawing when he noticed he was squirming in his seat. What was going on? It took a while to become aware of his body...and how badly he needed to pee.

He shifted again, hoping that a slightly different position would make it go away. He wanted to finish his drawing. When it only seemed to make things worse, he frowned. He didn't want to go to the bathroom, not when he was coloring. Once he got up and walked to the bathroom to pee, it would break his concentration, his flow. His brain would boot right up, and he'd be all distracted and squirrelly again.

He squirmed again, and then it hit him. He was wearing his diaper. Could he...? He closed his eyes for a second, imagining how it would feel. A little dirty and wrong, maybe, but Daddy would clean him if he asked. And Daddy would love it; that he did know.

He looked over his shoulder where Daddy sat on the couch, watching him. He knew. There was no doubt about it, he knew. With the smallest nod of his head, he encouraged Raf, but the choice was still his. No matter what he chose, Daddy would not be mad at him...and Daddy would love him.

What was the harm in doing it once, just to see if he liked it? If he didn't, he could always tell Daddy and never do it again. Daddy said it was okay if he didn't want it and still loved wearing a diaper. He couldn't make a wrong choice here.

His mind made up, he reached for his pencil again and colored in the baby dragon's right wing as he let go. He let out a breath of relief when he was done. Huh. His diaper felt full, heavier, but it wasn't as wet and gross as he had expected. Nodding in satisfaction, he went back to his coloring.

When he was done with the entire picture, he put his pencil down. "Daddy, I'm done!"

Daddy was beside him in a flash, sending him a proud smile that Raf felt in his soul. "Show me what you made, baby boy."

"I did the mama dragon. Isn't the baby the cutest? Look, I made him all purple."

"You did an amazing job, baby boy. And you chose such vibrant colors. Is it okay if I carefully cut this one out and hang it on the fridge?"

Raf had to blink a few times. "Yes, Daddy. I'd love that."

"What do you want to do next?" Daddy asked. He was giving Raf the choice to come clean or not.

He bit his lip. "I need a clean diaper, Daddy."

Daddy sunk to his knees in front of him. "I'm so, so proud of you for having done it, baby boy. Let Daddy clean you up, and then we can talk about how this made you feel."

The diaper definitely felt different when he walked. Heavy and full, and he didn't like that sensation. But when he lay down on the changing table, and the pure love in Daddy's eyes made him feel all warm inside.

"My sweet boy," Daddy praised him as he took the diaper off and cleaned him with wet wipes. "I'm so proud of you for letting go."

"It was because I didn't want to get up and lose my concentration with coloring."

Daddy smiled at him. "I know. I was watching you, wondering what you would do. How did it make you feel?"

"Relieved." Raf giggled. "It was not as wet and gross as I had expected. And I really like you cleaning me up. It's..." He scrunched his nose, trying to find words for how it made him feel, the way Daddy now cleaned him, spread new baby powder on him, and put on a fresh diaper. "It's like the highest level of intimacy. Even more intimate than sex."

Daddy nodded. 'I agree. There's a lot of trust and vulnerability involved."

He taped the diaper shut, then put Raf's onesie back on.

"I think I liked it, Daddy," Raf said as he sat up. "Not because of the peeing itself, but how it makes me feel to lie here, knowing you're taking care of me."

Daddy picked him up effortlessly. "I love you, baby boy. I couldn't love you more if I tried."

21

"Are you sure you don't want me to cancel?"

Brendan took a long, hard look at Raf's pale face, his eyes red-rimmed from crying.

"No. Please, Daddy, I want to go. It's Rhys. I can be myself with him, and Cornell is cool. He won't mind if I'm half in little-mode."

Brendan caressed Raf's cheek. "I'm gonna trust you on this, baby boy, but if I feel like it's too much for you, we're leaving. Rhys will understand that too. In hindsight, we shouldn't have planned this the day after your first therapy session."

Raf nodded. "I'm gonna go freshen up. Can I please wear a diaper, Daddy?"

Brendan hesitated. Rhys would be fine with it, that much he knew, but what about Cornell? The man was a sub, and he'd been one for many years, but that didn't mean he'd be accepting of all kinks. The last thing Raf needed right now was for someone to kink-shame him. Raf kept reassuring him Cornell was cool, so he'd just have to trust him.

"Okay. Call me when you're ready for me, baby boy."

Brendan watched him as he climbed up the stairs, his heart full of worry. He could understand Raf wanted him to meet Cornell, but the timing couldn't have sucked more. The first session had been rough on Raf. The therapist had been amazing, a warm, motherly woman who specialized in treating people with ADHD. Fifteen minutes in, she'd kindly told Raf that he seemed to be suffering from depression caused by childhood trauma, and Raf had taken it hard. He'd had a complete meltdown, crying so much Brendan had feared he'd never stop. God, it had hurt watching, even if he'd known it was necessary.

When Raf calmed down a bit, she'd told them that Raf had kept his emotions about his parents bottled up for so long he had a lot of catching up to do. It wouldn't be an easy road, she'd warned them, but she'd given Raf hope that he'd get through this. She also prepared him for the fact that his brain would be extra squirrelly the next day, a term that showed how much she understood about how Raf's mind worked.

Sadly, she'd been right. Raf had called him during lunch break, half in tears. Dolores had grown impatient with him after he'd made mistake after mistake. His day had only gotten worse after that, and Brendan had taken off work earlier to make sure he was home when Raf arrived. That had been the right decision. because he'd broken down as soon as he'd walked through the door.

It was too much for him, his full-time job in combination with his differences and now his depression, and the intense therapy he'd started. Something had to give, and Brendan kept mulling it over. This was an area where he had to tread lightly. Despite being Raf's Daddy, he couldn't make these big life decisions for him. They needed to have a talk about the future. This was not working.

When Raf called him upstairs, he rushed to him and put Raf's diaper on, and then they were off. It was a bit of a drive to the ranch where Rhys now lived, but it was a beautiful area with quiet country roads in rolling hills. Then again, Rhys's father had been killed on a quiet country road like that when an inexperienced driver skidded on a patch of black ice and hit his car head on. The snow had all melted by now, but Brendan still drove carefully.

"I'm so glad Cornell decided to stay with Rhys after he'd told him the truth," Raf said.

"I can't believe Rhys didn't tell him he was a Dom on the first day. Cornell had every right to be upset with him."

Raf had kept him posted on the confrontation between Rhys and Cornell. It had not gone over well, unsurprisingly. But Cornell had decided to stay for whatever reason, so now it was up to Rhys to make up for it. Brendan couldn't help but root for the guy, considering how long he'd apparently had the hots for Cornell. Love did strange things to a man, that much he understood.

"He doesn't know Rhys likes him, though."

Brendan smiled. "I know, baby boy. You told me a few times. I promise I won't say anything."

When they arrived, Rhys opened the door for them, greeting them with warm hugs. Raf practically bounced into the room. "It's so good to see you again," he told Cornell, who Brendan recognized from seeing him in a club once with Jonas.

"Raphael," Cornell said, his tone warm and welcoming. "Though if I remember correctly, you prefer to be called Raf, no?"

Raf gave him a happy smile. "Right. The only one who calls me Raphael is my Daddy when he's upset with me,"

Raf said, looking back at Brendan. Well, the cat was out of the bag now.

Cornell took a step toward him, then extended his hand. "Cornell. Very happy to meet you."

Brendan debated mentioning he'd already met him, but that would immediately bring up Jonas, so maybe he'd better not. "Brendan. Thanks so much for having us over."

They settled in the living room, Raf finding a spot at Brendan's feet. Cornell winced as he sat on the couch, rubbing his knee.

"Can I get you guys some drinks to start with?" Rhys asked.

Raf looked at Brendan. "Can I please have a glass of wine, Daddy?"

Brendan almost laughed that Raf would even ask. "Absolutely not. You remember what happened the last time you had alcohol?"

Raf's cute mouth pulled together into a pout. "Please, Daddy?"

"I said no, baby boy. Now stop whining, or you lose your bath privileges."

Raf's look changed into a contrite one, and he sent Brendan an apologetic look. "Apple juice, please."

"Do you want a regular glass or a sippy cup?"

God, Brendan wanted to kiss Rhys for asking, for even offering the option.

"The sippy cup, please, and thank you," Raf said with a happy smile.

Rhys took the rest of the drink orders, and when he had disappeared to the kitchen, Raf looked at Cornell. "Did Rhys tell you anything about me? About the relationship I have?"

Apparently, his boy had decided to tackle the whole

thing head on. It warmed his heart that Raf was being so brave.

"No, because he takes confidentiality seriously, but I kind of got the gist of it," Cornell said.

"We usually check with people to make sure it doesn't make them uncomfortable," Brendan said. "Raf tends to drop into little-mode when he's around people he trusts, like Rhys, but if you object to that in any way, we'll make sure to keep it limited."

Cornell chuckled. "Vanilla is boring. Please, be yourself. I've seen pretty much everything there is to see, so not only won't it shock me, but it doesn't bother me in the least either. I'm always happy to see people expressing their true selves."

"See, Daddy?" Raf said, his clear voice ringing through the room. "I told you Cornell was cool."

Brendan smiled at his boy. "Yes, you did, baby boy. But you know I'm always careful. I don't want you to get hurt."

Raf climbed onto his lap and snuggled against him, and Brendan instantly gathered him close. "That's why you are the best Daddy in the whole world."

Brendan kissed his head, too overwhelmed with love to even find words.

Rhys came back, carrying a tray with the drinks, which he handed out one by one. "Does he want to play for a little bit?" he asked Brendan.

"He had a rough day at work." Brendan didn't want to spill the beans about therapy—he wasn't sure what Raf was comfortable with—and he held Raf a little tighter. "If it wasn't for the fact that we knew you'd be okay with it, we would've canceled tonight because he really needs some time to relax."

Rhys nodded. "I figured as much. I'll get out some toys for him."

Rhys brought out the special rug he'd shown them before, as well as a bin of toy cars. Raf immediately slid off Brendan's lap and crawled over to the cars. "Here you go, buddy," Rhys said. "Have fun."

Seconds later, Raf was playing, lost to the world, and Brendan smiled with a deep sense of gratitude. "Thank you," he told Rhys. "I can't express how much it means to me."

Rhys shrugged. "My pleasure. I saw how stressed he was when you guys came in."

"So, what do you do in your daily life?" Brendan asked Cornell.

"I'm an estate lawyer," Cornell said. "So most of what I do is helping clients set up living wills, testaments, and handling their affairs after they've passed. And you?"

"I'm a real estate agent, but I also have several rental properties," Brendan said.

They chatted animatedly, conversation flowing easily while Raf played with his cars. Brendan handed him his sippy cup every now and then, wanting to make sure he had enough to drink, but other than that, he left him alone. Raf needed the downtime; that much was obvious.

Delicious smells wafted in from the kitchen. "Dinner will be ready in five minutes," Rhys told Brendan with a meaningful look.

Brendan nodded back. He wasn't surprised Rhys had also noticed that Raf had made use of his diaper, which meant he needed to be changed before sitting down for dinner.

Brendan got up from his seat and crouched down next to Raf. His hand found a spot on his head, caressing his curls.

"I'm sure you can play some more after dinner, but we need to get ready first."

Raf let out a little sigh but then leaned into Brendan's touch. "Yes, Daddy."

With Raf's hand in his, he walked into a guest bedroom Rhys had subtly pointed out. He'd even put a big towel on the bed so Brendan could take off Raf's diaper, and there was a package of wipes lying on the bed as well. The man was worth gold, Brendan thought, not for the first time.

Minutes later, Raf was cleaned and dressed again—sans diaper. Brendan hadn't brought a new one, which his boy was fine with. But when they walked back into the living room, they found Cornell plastered against Rhys, his whole body shaking with heavy sobs. Brendan shared a look with Rhys, who subtly shook his head.

"Let's go home, baby boy. I think these two need some privacy," he whispered.

"Do you think Cornell will be okay?" Raf asked in the car, his voice small.

"Grief is a hard process. He and Jonas were incredibly close, and it's going to take time to get through that. I lost one of my best friends in college after he took a stupid fall and a weak artery in his brain they never knew was there burst. It took months before I could think of him again without crying. Cornell will get there, and he's got Rhys, but it will take time."

Raf put his small hand on Brendan's thigh. "Like with me, right, Daddy?"

Brendan sent him a quick look. "Yes, like with you. Depression doesn't heal overnight, but you'll get there. And you know you have people supporting you every step of the way."

EPILOGUE

Six Months Later

"Daddy, look!"

Brendan smiled at the perfect handstand Raf did for him. "Nice job, baby boy!"

"I can do cartwheels too!"

Raf's voice carried through the garden, where Brendan sat with Rhys and Cornell, enjoying a beer while baby back ribs slow cooked on the grill. Luckily, Rhys was a much better grill master than Brendan's dad, and the smells wafting into his nose were delicious.

"He seems better," Rhys said.

"Much better," Brendan confirmed. "Therapy has been hard on him, but quitting his job was the best decision he ever made. He loves being home and doing the odd stuff for me, like building a new website or handling my email. He's actually quite good at that."

Rhys nodded. "His brain functions so much better when there's no pressure. The more pressure you put on him, the worse his symptoms get. I'm so glad he was able to quit. And I'm sure you love having him at your place permanently now."

Brendan grinned. "It's not like he was ever actually at his apartment, but I love that it's official now. Just like you guys, huh?"

Rhys shared a loving look with Cornell. "Just like us."

Brendan hadn't been surprised in the least to learn that a few weeks ago Rhys and Cornell were in a Daddy-boy relationship as well. Rhys had shown all the instincts of an awesome Daddy already with Raf all those years, and apparently he'd felt the same nurturing care toward Cornell. It was amazing to see them together, so in tune and harmonious you could feel the love in the room.

Not that he and Raf were any different. His boy had bloomed under his care, and things were perfect between the two of them. Raf now volunteered with his mom at the hospital and spent every Friday afternoon with his dad, learning how to build things from wood.

Brendan had been worried at first that Raf would hurt himself, but once he'd watched the endlessly patient way his dad instructed Raf and made sure he was safe, he'd let go. Raf loved spending time with them, and the parental love he soaked up like a little baby plant made him grow and shine brighter every day.

Things with Raf's parents were tense. His dad had contacted him out of the blue, but Raf refused to speak to him, blocking his number. He'd tried again through his mom, whom Raf spoke to occasionally, and he'd told her that if she tried to reconcile him and his dad again, she, too, would lose him. Things hadn't been the same since, but for Raf, it brought freedom.

"When are you thinking of making things even more official?" Rhys teased.

Brendan smiled, lifting an eyebrow. "You're asking me about my intentions, *Daddy*?"

Rhys sent him a cheeky grin. "I gotta look out for my boys."

"You take care of your own boy." Brendan nodded at Cornell, who watched them with amusement in his eyes. "I've got this one."

He hesitated for a second but then took the small box out of his pocket, showing it to Rhys and Cornell when he was sure Raf wasn't watching. Rhys's mouth dropped open, and Brendan put it back.

"How long have you been walking around with that?" Rhys whispered.

"Two weeks now, but it'll end tomorrow night. I considered doing some grand proposal, but that's not us."

"What did you plan?" There was a wistfulness in Cornell's tone.

"We're invited for dinner at my parents tomorrow, and I'm gonna do it there. They have no idea, and neither does Raf, but I know I'll make three people happy."

"Four," Rhys said. "I promise you you'll never regret marrying him. He's the best friend I could ever have, and you're damn lucky to have him."

Brendan watched Raf as he did another cartwheel on the grass, then tumbled down when he tripped. His carefree laughter rose up to the sky.

Brendan leaned back in his chair, his heart so full it felt like it was about to burst. "I'm the luckiest man on the planet."

. . .

THE END

Do you want to read how Daddy pushes Raf's boundaries? Check out this delicious FREE bonus scene!

FREEBIES

If you love FREE novellas and bonus chapters, head on over to my website where I offer bonus scenes for several of my books, as well as as two free novellas. Grab them here: http://www.noraphoenix.com/free-bonus-scenes-novellas/

BOOKS BY NORA PHOENIX

🎧 indicates book is also available as audio book

Perfect Hands Series

Raw, emotional, both sweet and sexy, with a solid dash of kink, that's the Perfect Hands series. All books can be read as standalones.

- **Firm Hand** (daddy care with a younger daddy and an older boy) 🎧
- **Gentle Hand** (sweet daddy care with age play) 🎧
- **Naughty Hand** (a holiday novella to read after Firm Hand and Gentle Hand)

No Shame Series

If you love steamy MM romance with a little twist, you'll love the No Shame series. Sexy, emotional, with a bit of suspense and all the feels. Make sure to read in order, as this is a series with a continuing storyline.

- **No Filter** 🎧

- **No Limits** 🎧
- **No Fear** 🎧
- **No Shame** 🎧
- **No Angel** 🎧

And for all the fun, grab the **No Shame box set** 🎧 which includes all five books plus exclusive bonus chapters and deleted scenes.

Irresistible Omegas Series

An mpreg series with all the heat, epic world building, poly romances (the first two books are MMMM and the rest of the series is MMM), a bit of suspense, and characters that will stay with you for a long time. This is a continuing series, so read in order.

- **Alpha's Sacrifice**
- **Alpha's Submission**
- **Beta's Surrender**
- **Alpha's Pride**
- **Beta's Strength**
- **Omega's Protector**
- **Alpha's Obedience**
- **Omega's Power**

Ballsy Boys Series

Sexy porn stars looking for real love! Expect plenty of steam, but all the feels as well. They can be read as standalones, but are more fun when read in order.

- **Ballsy** (free prequel)
- **Rebel** 🎧
- **Tank** 🎧

- **Heart** 🎧
- **Campy** 🎧
- **Pixie** 🎧

Kinky Boys Series

More sexy porn stars! This is a kinky spin off from the Ballsy Boys, set in Las Vegas.

- **Daddy**

Ignite Series

An epic dystopian sci-fi trilogy (one book out, two more to follow) where three men have to not only escape a government that wants to jail them for being gay but aliens as well. Slow burn MMM romance.

- **Ignite** 🎧
- **Smolder**

Stand Alones

I also have a few stand alones, so check these out!

- **Kissing the Teacher** (sexy daddy kink between a college prof and his student. Age gap, no ABDL) 🎧
- **The Time of My Life** (two men meet at a TV singing contest)
- **Shipping the Captain** (falling for the boss on a cruise ship)
- **Snow Way Out** (snowed in, age gap, size difference, and a bossy twink)

MORE ABOUT NORA PHOENIX

Would you like the long or the short version of my bio?

The short? You got it.

I write steamy gay romance books and I love it. I also love reading books. Books are everything.

How was that?

A little more detail? Gotcha.

I started writing my first stories when I was a teen...on a freaking typewriter. I still have these, and they're adorably romantic. And bad, haha. Fear of failing kept me from following my dream to become a romance author, so you can imagine how proud and ecstatic I am that I finally overcame my fears and self doubt and did it. I adore my genre because I love writing and reading about flawed, strong men who are just a tad broken..but find their happy ever after anyway.

My favorite books to read are pretty much all MM/gay romances as long as it has a happy end. Kink is a plus... Aside from that, I also read a lot of nonfiction and not just books on writing. Popular psychology is a favorite topic of mine and so are self help and sociology.

Hobbies? Ain't nobody got time for that. Just kidding. I love traveling, spending time near the ocean, and hiking. But I love books more.

Come hang out with me in my Facebook Group Nora's Nook where I share previews, sneak peeks, freebies, fun stuff, and much more: https://www.facebook.com/groups/norasnook/

My weekly newsletter not only gives you updates, exclusive content, and all the inside news on what I'm working on, but also lists the best new releases, 99c deals, and freebies in gay romance for that weekend. Load up your Kindle for less money! Sign up here: http://www.noraphoenix.com/newsletter/

You can also stalk me on Twitter: @NoraFromBHR

On Instagram:

https://www.instagram.com/nora.phoenix/

On Bookbub:

https://www.bookbub.com/profile/nora-phoenix

Made in the USA
Coppell, TX
11 April 2021

53407370R00135